P9-AGQ-038

Surviving Adverse Seasons

ILLINOIS SHORT FICTION

Crossings by Stephen Minot
A Season for Unnatural Causes by Philip F. O'Connor
Curving Road by John Stewart
Such Waltzing Was Not Easy by Gordon Weaver

Rolling All the Time by James Ballard
Love in the Winter by Daniel Curley
To Byzantium by Andrew Fetler
Small Moments by Nancy Huddleston Packer

One More River by Lester Goldberg
The Tennis Player by Kent Nelson
A Horse of Another Color by Carolyn Osborn
The Pleasures of Manhood by Robley Wilson, Jr.

The New World by Russell Banks
The Actes and Monuments by John William Corrington
Virginia Reels by William Hoffman
Up Where I Used to Live by Max Schott

The Return of Service by Jonathan Baumbach
On the Edge of the Desert by Gladys Swan
Surviving Adverse Seasons by Barry Targan
The Gasoline Wars by Jean Thompson

Surviving Adverse Seasons

Stories by Barry Targan

UNIVERSITY OF ILLINOIS PRESS

Urbana Chicago London

Manufactured in the United States of America

"Kingdoms," *Sewanee Review*, vol. 86, no. 3, Summer, 1978

"The Garden," *Salmagundi*, no. 46, Fall, 1979

"The Rags of Time," *Southwest Review*, vol. 64, no. 3, Summer, 1979

"Surviving Adverse Seasons," *Salmagundi*, nos. 31-32, Fall, 1975-Winter, 1976; reprinted in *Best American Short Stories* (1976).

Library of Congress Cataloging in Publication Data

Targan, Barry, 1932—
Surviving adverse seasons.
(Illinois short fiction)
I. Title.
PZ4.T184Su [PS3570.A59] 813'.5'4 79-20191
ISBN 0-252-00786-7
ISBN 0-252-00787-5 pbk.

To Ronnie

Contents

Kingdoms

I

My father is somewhere in America, parked in his pick-up at a campsite if he is south, where it is still warm enough to sleep outside under blankets. Or else, if he is north, he is in a cheap hotel in, say, Duluth, in one of those just-off-of-center-city hotels for those who need them. And my father would know them all.

My father is somewhere in America, if nothing has happened to him, as at any moment it might. The last I heard from him was from Topeka. That was four months ago. He called, collect. "Nothing has changed," he said. Whatever else he said—about his health, the condition of the pick-up, the price of clear pine or of copper tubing in Topeka, the weather—what he really called to say was that "Nothing has changed." Not that he expected it to. Not that I did.

When I was ten my mother died in an automobile accident, in a car tumbled across a highway by a blown tire. The Vermont State Police reconstructed the accident for us. For my father, rather. He told me about it later. For twenty-five years I have, from time to time, come crashing out of sleep shouting to her to jump, to live. But she did not.

In 1950, when my mother died, my father was professor of English at Amherst College. He was forty-two and had written three books—about Shakespeare, about Ben Jonson, and about a late seventeenth-century poet of whom nearly no one had heard at that time, Thomas Traherne. My father is supposed to have made him, Traherne, well known. He had also written countless articles about the literature of the sixteenth and seventeenth centuries. Everything he wrote someone would print. And he ranged more widely, too, and could discourse extempore on the latest fiction and poetry or on anything else—boats, painting, butterflies. He had a mighty sweep. He told me all this, *taught* it to me, in all the strange and gorgeous years we shared. After.

In 1951, a year after my mother's death, Milton Carswell, a man only two years younger than my father, married with two children, and a specially good friend of my father's, was rejected for tenure after six years at Amherst.

For other men it might have gone on differently—gone on, at least, at another school or even as an insurance salesman, even as a waiter. But Milton Carswell, by forty, had been broken to the belief that his only true goal in life was to get a job and then to keep it for life. He did not know that about himself until it was too late. He should have worked for civil service, but he became a teacher of Shelley's poetry and Keats's instead. At forty, Milton Carswell, after too many schools, had been judged by the caprice of his profession too long, had been evaluated one time too many, had been weighed in the ever-fining scales beyond his capacity for extension. There was nothing left of him. He had been ground too small, and when the worst wind that his shriveled life had taught him to think he could dream of actually did come, he blew away.

After all the orderly appeals (led by my father) to the various committees were over, after the student demonstrations and the offers of good letters of recommendation from those who had fired him, and after the party at which everybody got drunk and happy like stoic Romans bred out of risible Greeks, after all that, Milton Carswell put his affairs in order and killed himself. No one knew he even had a gun. So few in college have. Perhaps Milton Carswell, wiser by experience in his profession's ways, attuned to them, had prepared.

That was in February. Soon after, my father requested and got a leave of absence for the following year. In late May he bought a pick-up truck and began building it into a movable aluminum house. In those days there were no luxurious, fully equipped pods that you could buy in one hour and back up under and then in one hour drive off, ready to plug in anywhere. And in those days there were no places to plug into. If you traveled the land, then you traveled it on its terms.

My father could use his hands. He worked seven days a week on his truck, building it, modifying it. Long days. At night he charted courses like a navigator on maps. In the middle of June, a dragging week more of my school to go, my father told me his plan. The day after school was over for me, we were going to drive west, across America. Take all summer to do it. The Grand Canyon, Mount Rushmore, Death Valley—I had only to name it.

At eleven I was ready for such a grand adventure, but I was not yet ready to give up my chance as starting pitcher for my Little League team.

I wasn't sure, I told him, that I wanted to go. I mean I told him that I wanted to go but that I wanted to pitch, too. And what about the Y camp in August? For the only time in my life, then or after, he told me I must do what he had decided. So it was settled. On June 23 we drove west on Route 9 out of town, our first destination Chicago, our first stop that day wherever the night caught us.

We never went back.

I mean we never went back to Amherst, to 312 Chelsea Street to a place called home. We went back physically five years later, but as visitors, caravaneers passing through as we had passed through so many other places. I was sixteen and little had changed except me. When the decision had come to sell the house, to cut out completely, I think we were in Salt Lake City, about forty miles south of it on the farthest fringe of the lake. My father had arranged the sale of the house, the sale of much that was in it, the packing and sending to a sister in Harrisburg, Pennsylvania, of what was left, all by telephone and a few letters.

Driving slowly down Chelsea Street that summer day, we stopped nowhere, spoke to no one. And how could I have begun to tell them what had happened?

"Sooner or later," he would tell me, by firelight (where it was good to hear him, whatever he said), or over the hot plate that he lugged about to cook our supper on in the crummy hotel rooms (which I hated), "Sooner or later," he would shout at me, me sitting on the side of the large high single bed we would sleep in together, my feet dangling two inches above the floor, "Sooner or later," he would wave his wooden cooking spoon about, would stir the beans, slice the hard, dark breads he could always find in whatever city we came to, butter it thick for me, hand me a carrot, boil a knockwurst, pour out a jelly glass of milk, "Sooner or later all our corpuscles are bursting and rotting one by one. Our neurons atrophy second by second. Tick-tock, kid. Tick-tock, my little warrior." Then he would turn from me and weep. My own sorrow for him then was infinite, though I could not name it or comprehend it.

At the end of supper, after the few dishes (washed in the hallway bathroom), we would play chess. Or listen to the radio, listening, between each country and western song, to the distant pounding voices from Del Rio, Texas, or Wheeling, West Virginia, selling illustrated Rembrandt Bibles bound in white gold-embossed calfskin or two-foot-high carved imitation onyx crucifixes with simulated ivory Jesuses hanging upon them. TV was only beginning and was not ordinary, and where we stayed it would never be available except in the lobby of stuffed armchairs and spring-sprung sofas with dazed old men fraying apart in them.

Or else, and frequently, he would read to me. Sometimes he would read to me a book my equal: *Call of the Wild* or *Greatest Baseball Players of the Century.* But mostly, too impatient for the deceptions of children's literature, anxious for the great deceptions, he would read to me from his own vaster store. He would read, complete with commentary, say, from *Hamlet:*

> And let me speak to the yet unknowing world
> How these things came about: so shall you hear
> Of carnal, bloody, and unnatural acts,
> Of accidental judgements, casual slaughters,

Of deaths put on by cunning and forced cause,
And, in this upshot, purposes mistook
Fall'n on the inventors' heads: all this can I
Truly deliver.

"How about that, my young friend? How about that?"

What he meant was that nothing was bitter enough. Nothing that he had taught back in Amherst, nothing that the greatest artists wrote, none of it prepared us for the terribleness of our dispossessed lives, our unaccommodated lives.

"Literature is too redemptive," he would shout, hunched over the wheel of the truck in the earlier, increasingly manic years.

Suffering was his theme.

By the end of the first summer, too close to the end of it for me reasonably to get back east in time for school, we had circled out of Seattle, climbed the switchbacked roads and then trails up the Cascades and rolled down the eastern slope of them into the slowly drying basin of what becomes central Washington. We stopped for a week in Walla Walla. That was where my father did his first skilled labor, tested, I think, the possibility of the life he came at last to lead.

We had stopped for our lunch on some boundary of Walla Walla where the city feathered into countryside. In the morning, before we set out, he would make sandwiches and often a thermos of soup so when we stopped at noon, or whenever, we were ready. But it was not time he was trying to save; later I saw that it was time he was trying to spend.

That day we were eating lunch in a small park, the remnant of a larger woods that had been trimmed down and left to be surrounded by the dozens of houses and hundreds of people coming quickly. All through our lunch my father was uncharacteristically silent. We had been following baseball through the summer and guessing at it as the pennant races drew down to October and the series. I had carried across the continent all my baseball cards and had added to them at every opportunity through the land. We talked baseball a lot. The same things. He would tell me the same stories of his young baseball adventures, and I would give him statistics. I would quote extensively the facts of baseball printed on the backs of cards in type too small for any but the youngest eyes to see or care about.

But that day in Walla Walla we sat in the tiny park and did not talk. We ate silently as he looked across at the men who were building the houses, who had also stopped working to eat. When we had finished and they had finished, he got up and walked over into the clutter of the project, the skeletons of studs and rafters and joists and headers that looked more handsome in their honesty than would the gimcrackery that would be hoisted upon them. I had been with him when he had done that before, had walked with him as he observed and muttered at the shabbiness, at the fraud of the buildings. They would not last a generation, he told me, but I did not know how long a generation was.

Today was different. He found the man who seemed to be managing the site and asked him for a job. And he got it. The houses had to be finished before the winter, before the snow, which, in that high plateau of the country, came early.

He began work the next morning, crawling across sheets of plyscore, hammering them onto the rafters for the roof. On that first day I waited down below. After each roof he and the crew he worked in would move down the row to the next house. I would follow, watch them climb up the ladder, listen to the hammer bursts of nailing, and wait. I could not think what else to do. It was the first time I had been alone. He had not talked much that night about his taking the job. He may not have known himself what to say.

But on the second day I sought my own necessities. I was eleven, getting on toward twelve and a good size for my age. And I had had a summer on the road by now. New places did not stop me as they had earlier. All my places by now were new.

That second day, Wednesday, I walked down the rise from the housing project farther into the city, keeping to Lincoln Avenue like a thread raveling out behind me so that I would know my way back. In fifteen long blocks I came to a schoolyard where boys were playing, throwing a basketball up against the wall to where a hoop should be, but there was none. They passed off, drove hard for the basket, hooked or leaped up for arching one-handers and scored or did not score by measurements or agreements of their own. I did not know why they were not in school. And I do not remember wondering then. Perhaps I simply assumed that they were like me, of that band afloat now in a sea of different circumstance, no longer moored—or tethered—to places like home or school. Or games like others played.

They were all older than I, around fifteen I'd guess, maybe more. They played hard, and sometimes a team would win and a new game would start. I watched carefully for nearly an hour, coming closer, until I was noticed.

"You want to play?" the tallest boy asked me. "You want to play?"

"I don't know how," I said.

"You don't know how to play basketball?"

"I don't know how to play without the hoop."

"It's easy," he said. "Here." He pushed the ball at me very hard and it bounced painfully off my fingers. I picked the ball up.

"Shoot," he commanded. I lofted the ball as best I could to where the basket should have been. "Terrific," he shouted. "Great shot. You're on my team." So we began. But with or without a true hoop, I could not play with them. They were too large and fast for me, but more: they were playing a different game, different even from the imaginary game I had watched. For I was the game. The center of the circle. "It," the flag to capture, the creature to be run.

The ball bounced off my head. I turned. I was hit with the ball from the other side. I turned there and was hit again from behind.

"Come on, man," my captain shouted. "Get with it. Hang onto the ball, man. How we going to make a play without the ball?" And I would be hit. They ringed me with laughter. I did not try to move through them, though no one offered to bar me.

I stood the thudding of the ball as an animal in shock will wait for the net of ravening hunters to close in upon it, and not outrun them as it might. How could I end what I could not comprehend? Until I turned once in time to see the ball come. I caught it and threw it hard like a baseball into his face, smashing his nose. After his scream, after his blood, they moved at me with their fists, kicking, punching.

And then they were gone, like a squall that can come on a perfect day and break down trees and strip the blossoms in a garden, batter wheat with hail and go as quickly, leaving the day as perfect, perhaps even clearer, brighter, as still. I was in the schoolyard, not too damaged, alone. I walked out onto Lincoln Avenue and began the long, slow, easy climb up out of the city to its edge.

What had touched me? How could I imagine what had happened, me, this child of perfect peace? I would ask my father. He who knew everything, would know. He would tell me. But when I got back to the construction site I found him waiting for me by our truck, beaten too.

His lip was split and blood was crusted on it. His left eye was red and puffy. The top two buttons of his work shirt were popped off, the collar slightly ripped. When I saw him, only then did I cry. But when he saw me, bruised and cracked myself, and understood as I told him, sobbing, about my own wounds, he laughed, rose up and whooped to heaven.

"Omens, little friend," he said to me, his arm across my shoulder. "Portents. Auguries." He got water from the truck and washed my face, opened a beer from our cooler and poured me some and drank the rest. Then we set off, slowly, down my Lincoln Avenue, past the now-empty schoolyard, into the center of Walla Walla and across it and toward the south.

"What's in Oregon?" he asked at a crossroad. "Pick something." I had the map.

"Pendleton. It's about sixty miles. It's right on a main road."

So that is where we went, to a small aspen grove of a state campsite just above the city where through the October night, all night, great machines roared westward and north across the sky protecting us.

By our small fire he told me that he had slipped on the roof and had dropped his hammer on a man, on the man's shoulder, and the man came up onto the roof to fight him. The man would accept no apology, no explanation. Even after the brief fight, the man would have no containment, no calm, as if the accident, so close to being worse, to maybe killing him, had stained him, violated him irreparably. He was angry like a madman. But he was not mad. The foreman settled him by sending him off the job for the rest of the day. He fired my father. It was a solution.

And as my father told me this, expanding what he told, elaborating, recalling, noting and annotating the way a scholar might upon a myth, he would nod briefly, fiercely. To his own incident and perception he added my bizarre attack, mixing and mumbling incantations like an alchemist amidst his limbecks and retorts, approaching distillation. Then, like the embers in our little fire, he glowed and brightened and at last burst into renewed flame, a harrowing wind blowing through him forever.

"Now might I do it pat," he cracked across the night so that I stood up at that stabbing sound. "And now I'll do it." He raised his arms to the stars. "Be thou my good," he said, not to the stars he gestured at, but to vaster intelligences. I was frightened. And not frightened. Thrilled, rather. Enamoured. He was marvelous, if baffling, but attuned to regions beyond me, I was sure. I had faith. "Go pee," he said to me.

He helped me into my bunk in the truck and told me my nighttime story. Not that it was always a tale; sometimes it was history or theories of bird migration and such, or poems. Sometimes he sang. But from the beginning of time, my time, he had always been there to tell me something. Tonight he told me of someone called Actaeon, a great hunter, who chanced to look upon the goddess Artemis while she was bathing—alas, a sin. In punishment she turned Actaeon into a stag so that his own hounds turned on him, pursued, and killed him.

"It isn't fair," I said as I sank down. "It wasn't his fault."

"Precisely," my father said. "Yes. Exactly." He gripped my hand tight, hard with his excitement about his own understanding and what he thought was mine. "But remember this." His whisper was like a knife. "The gods are not just. But they are *right.*" But even if I had understood, I was too tired to care; so even if he was telling me one of life's enormous and valuable secrets, I would have to learn it again in other ways, in a different time, not now. Then he leaned over me and kissed my forehead as always. Always.

In the morning he explained that I was to stay by myself for this day and night and part of the next day. We set up a tent, arranged what needed arranging, and he drove off. He told me I would be all right. Just stay put. And don't worry.

I read and walked about the aspen grove, sat by a small stream watching late striders on the autumn-low water of the pond, made my supper and went into the tent early. He returned the following morning by eleven o'clock.

"Let's go. Move it." In twenty minutes we were packed up and gone. To Boise eastward, I think, or maybe farther.

After ten miles he told me what he had done. "I joined up," he said. "We enlisted in the war. I went back to Walla Walla and broke his truck. Ah, the daring of it! When they were on the last house I opened his hood and worked an acid paste into his distributor, some on the coil, here and there in other spots. In a day, maybe two, his truck will need a lot of fixing. I did it. Me." He looked sideways at me as the land rose and fell and rose all about us, stiffening into Idaho and the Rockies. "Do you know what I did?" he asked.

"Sure. You told me just now. The truck."

"No. Not that. More. Deeper. More important. Listen! Listen! I did a small and petty thing. A vicious thing. Me. And I am *pleased* by that. *An irrevocable act of violence on my own.* Now let's see what it's like, huh? Right? From now on?"

"What what's like?" I asked. But he did not answer that, or even hear it, I think. He hunched up over the steering wheel and squinted out, smiling. If he could have answered what I asked, we might have driven other roads. Or nowhere. But he could not answer me. That is what we were to seek. That is why.

II

For three years we traveled in a great swooping peregrination of this country—Lincoln, Wichita, Little Rock—like a soaring bird in the buffeting wind of his necessity. We rose on the thermals of his excitement, we fell through low valleys—Minneapolis, Lexington, Charleston, or Flagstaff or Carson City. We traveled north or east as the gusts sweeping through him took us, settling from time to time to work or to observe or for my father to recapitulate, to gather up his evidences and refine his briefs against life and its chronicles in these, the assizes of our existence, where the judges were his own Furies. And yet not fury, not anger; more a furiousness, the passionateness of accomplishment, really, and not frustration; for what had compelled him out of Amherst and the sinecure of his living still sustained him now. Each day he found a renewing marvel in being right, in being free now to be right.

In those years he was like a wire singing and hot with the energy of countless messages crowding and blazing through it. For him, his verifications were everywhere: the poets had failed—the first hard cutting wave of mind upon oblivion, the last phalanx of civilized defense. All for naught.

"But not us, kiddo. None of the monkdom of literature for us, right? No easy outs. Here is where we are now living, right smack in the world's wind, taking this chill from it right into the bones to give the lie in the teeth to consciousness, which doth make cowards of us all. Yes," he would emphasize, smacking his spoon upon a log or table top, his tin cup of wine upon a rock. "Listen to this." Then he would recite to me or read to me from books—stories, poems, plays, poking at the texts with his finger and poking through their misinforming fabric. Perhaps he read or recollected too selectively, allowing his fierce argument to follow a convenient vein; but on balance I think not. From singing Homer to the strident present, pessimism, despair, the bitterness of the primary truth of the human condition—it was all diluted, attenuated either in religious faiths or ideologies and their assumptions of order and equity, or in the "Blakean humpty-dump of the personal vision," as he styled it. But at the critical point, in the fell crunch of circumstance, writer after writer backed off, accepted some validating moral structure in the universe, insisted upon or suggested *some* reason for it all, this progress of a mortal soul upon this thoroughfare of woe.

"This thoroughfare of woe," he bellowed. "Chaucer," he told me. "That comes close. Chaucer nearly makes it sometimes." He told me about Alison sticking her brazen ass out into the night and immortality. "The *comic* sense. That's maybe all you can trust. There are others," he would nod wisely, knowingly. "Moments, lines, stanzas, chapters, something here and there. But nothing altogether. No. At the edge of truth's abyss, they all step back, even Willie S. But not us, huh, bub? Now that we know?" Then he would reach over and put his hand on me somewhere—my knee, my arm, my head—and leave it there, forgetting it, content only then.

And so he would lecture on. Reading, declaiming, interpreting, haranguing, wrenching apart the heartstrung words of man, stridently arguing me to his side, determined that I, at least, should make no mistake about it, and certainly not repeat his. But if he told me the stories about which he fumed and railed, so too did we create tales of our own. And gather others.

We evolved a method of existing. For about a year at first we would drive around in whatever community we found ourselves until he located a construction site—a single house going up, or a shopping center, or even more often somebody repairing storm windows or the steps to his front porch. Or working on his car. My father would inquire, offer, bargain, and surprisingly he would get the work, at least enough, replacing someone who had not shown up on the job, or by knowing what to do just when the homeowner or car repairer did not. And he worked cheaply—an enticement to a crew chief, who could keep the difference between my father's wages and what was recorded. Unions posed an obstacle, especially in large constructions, but even then there were ways around them. There were always ways around, and other ways. I think that is what my father wanted to know and to prove. Certainly. Perfectly. The non-Euclidean necessity to human action, the negativity of moral space.

Later on he refined his methods. We would walk about until he found a problem—a broken gate, dangling gutters, a pane of glass that was cracked or needed reglazing. He would ring the bell and make his offer, a clean, well-mannered man and his apprentice. We were seldom refused the work. And after, once he had done his first job, then chairs with loose rungs were found, dripping faucets, doors that stuck. And he would fix them, learning much as he went along, but learning quickly.

Frequently we were fed. And interrogated. He would invent, sometimes so wildly that I would go out to the truck with my wonder, embarrassment, and laughter at who he had turned us into—the two of us displaced in a hundred ways by fate in a thousand guises: the loss of the farm, the depletion of our marginal gold mine, the burning down of the small hardware business, the crash of our independent cargo delivery airplane, even the sinking of our fishing boat. From all our disasters we were striking out anew, crossing to a new coast for a new start.

More and more I came to wait for the history he would create for us, excited to know who we were now, this time, what we had passed through, where we had been, where we were going. Some of those fragments that he quickly hewed out of thin air I wished I had been; they seemed then so substantial to me, sharply faceted with details of purpose, carved with a point and direction to their movement.

And his auditors were unfailingly distressed, but heartened, too. We were brave events for them, and they seldom asked more than he told—as if the privilege of intimacy had already been too great, and was a gift not to be abused, but to be somehow reciprocated. Often I was given good clothing, shoes, books, games—so much that my father would sell it at thrift shops along our twisting course.

Outside in our truck, driving off, he would present me his latest evidence. "Fiction," he would shout. "See what it does?"

So we beat on, sometimes driving a thousand hard miles in two days, sometimes roaming softly through a small district for a week or even more. Mostly we avoided the larger cities, where it was expensive to live on the edge of things. And less pleasant and more dangerous. But he insisted that nothing be totally avoided, and that for us to take a different road for a good reason was as fruitless as it had been for Oedipus to flee Corinth to his doom. Thus I came to Sophocles. I remember objecting to the riddle of the Sphinx. I thought it was a dumb riddle. "It could of been something else. I mean the answer didn't *have* to be Man." At that he quickly swerved to the roadside, stopped the truck, and clasped my head into his arms. "Oh right, oh, yes," he said. I could hardly breathe. "Oh what a sweetheart. Oh what a head have I got here." And he squeezed me until I gasped and cried out. And giggled, cross and amazed at the same time. He was irresistible.

As in St. Louis. In August, along the low, river-level bank of St. Louis, we drove slowly up an industrial street called Fillion Place, looking for a used auto parts store he had located in the yellow pages. He needed a throw-out bearing for our clutch, which was beginning to slip badly. Fillion Place was grimy and black, buildings and windows so deeply stained and crusted by carbon exhaust and oil that even on the sunniest days the light was absorbed out of the air, leaving a husk of gloom. Delivery trucks were all around, in the street and on the thin sidewalk. Steel drums of substances and crates were piled up, intermixed with refuse and strewn packaging. In the air was a seamless sound of gears and motors and tailgates banging and voices ordering things about.

Near where the auto parts store should have been, a small explosion blew out a second-floor window, white steam sprayed out in a rolling billow and died to a small hiss, even as the last glass pattered and tinkled to the ground and onto our truck. A man in a clean summery business suit ran out of the building, looked up and down Fillion Place, which had noticed nothing, and then up at the window. Then he saw us.

"What do you want? What are you looking at? Go on, get out of here." He turned back to the shattered window and the thin stream. "Jesus," he said.

"You want it fixed or not?" my father said.

"What?" the man said, turning again. "You some kind of wise guy? Go on, get out of here."

"I fix things. I can fix that."

"Listen," the man said. "One more time. Get out of here."

But my father got out of the truck. The man jumped back, frightened. He started to raise his hands as if my father had threatened to hit him. "Whaa," he croaked.

"I've got to buy a part," my father said, and pointed to the store two buildings down. Trucks shook by. He walked away. I watched the man. He leaned back against the building, looking down at his shoes. The steam was falling against the building, condensing in a long wet black sharply pointed tongue descending the wall. If he did not move soon, the black slick would pierce him. At the last instant he came over to the truck.

"Is that your father?"

"Yes."

"What's he do?"

"He fixes things."

"What's that mean?"

"We drive around fixing things, working." I pointed into the back of our truck, at the heavy arrangement of tools and materials.

"That's all you do? Anywhere?"

"That's all." I explained a little more. The man walked back to the wall and began to pace. When my father came out of the store, the man approached him. They talked and concluded. I had seen it many times before.

We unloaded the tools my father selected and locked up the truck and started for the building.

"Leave the boy," the man said, but my father would not.

The second floor we mounted to was a distillery, a perfect small bootleg operation, as my father would later explain.

The rest is mostly small confusions that jigsaw together in my memory. I remember the man hovering about my father and arguing with him about everything, at every move—turning off the steam, opening certain valves, making other adjustments.

Still, the work went on. I wandered about between hundred-pound sacks of sugar piled twenty high, drums of malt extract stenciled in New Jersey, wooden boxes of aluminum-foil-wrapped blocks of dried yeast. At the very rear of the warehouse some kind of grain, maybe wheat, stood in a mountain with its peak touching the trap door it must have been dumped from. Rats scurried in and around the grain. I ran back to the apparatus of tubing and closed vessels and boilers.

My father was working in and around the whole thing. The man had removed his coat; his shirt was soaked and sticking completely to his skin, making him ghostly pink and glowing. He was urging him to hurry, but as my father worked, he talked. He asked questions about the distillery, made comments about how to improve the operation, expressed his admiration for it all. The man grew angry at the talk. My father provoked him.

"You're crazy," he said to my father, "talking so much. You should hurry up and get out of here. You're in trouble just being here now, let me tell you. You know that? You can figure that out, can't you?"

But my father persisted, wondering what label, if any, they used, and how they handled distribution.

Then the other men came. They argued among themselves. My father told me softly to get over to the stairs. Then the tangle of pipes and vats and spigots blew apart, or, more accurately, cracked open at a dozen turns and points. Steam, alcohol fumes, ambrosial yeastiness puffed through the warehouse and out into Fillion Place. I scrambled down the stairs, my father thudding behind me. Into the truck, careening down Fillion Place, up into St. Louis, through it, past it, beyond it, my father was whooping, slapping on the steering wheel.

"We're on the lam," he shouted. "The gang is after us."

I looked behind. He might have been right. I did not see why he should not have been right.

"Fugitives," he hollered, delighted. "Outlaws. Marked by the Mafia. Beyond the Pale. Wanted men. Godalmighty," he yipped in his pleasure and wonderment. "Talk about luck." He tooted the horn. We did not stop until Columbia. And then not again until Odessa, on our way to Kansas City.

III

Who was my father now from whom he had been? I remember that when my mother was alive my father was a quiet man, but not subdued or scholarly in that sense, or pale and soft and silent. He had always been active, busy, a good companion for talking or fishing, and sometimes exuberant. But he was reflective, quiet that way, as if he was always looking at and through what he was saying, or hearing, considering and adjusting his thoughts within an elegant context, a splendid fretwork of infinite but controlled complexity. And I remember him from Amherst days as being orderly and neat in his affairs, efficient and economical, yet without being overbearing and pinched about it: precise, I suppose, in the way of strong and confident men. There was a constant *tone* about him, and I battened in the safety and constancy. My mother's energy and urgency lit my life against and through the firm foil and lens of my father. There were no dark corners then.

He was, I think now, in those early days on Chelsea Street, a man who had made up his mind early, who had come to all his conclusions once and for all. He was a man who had used his good and well-furnished mind, his bright humor and excellent health, to examine the principle of things, the *grain* of ideas, the *weft* of thought, and thus could live abundantly in that illumination. And calmly, open minded but certain. Sure.

So it was not, either simply or complexly, the deaths of my mother and Milton Carswell, precipitants though they were, that caused or sustained this new extension. For in an important way I do not think he changed. I think he continued to examine as ever the principle of things, the grain and weft, but came, because of his strengths of spirit and qualities of mind, to a new perception of the universe so staggeringly different from his early conclusions and desires that the joy of his wonder and the consequence of his rage could not help but follow, as if a man of his attainments had no other choice. Given a place to stand, a fulcrum and a lever long enough, Archimedes claimed that he could move the earth. Now my father believed that he had found such a place, such a fulcrum, and day by day he thought to prove again that proposition, explore its ramifications, develop corollaries, and nudge the planet inch by inch into another orbit.

But there is more to any explanation of my father's behavior: there was the expiation he demanded for his special guilt of having ever accepted the artificial mysteries of the arranged—*nice*—ambiguities of literature and the hope engendered. So he also set out to atone for that faith, to fathom mystery truly now by becoming a part of mystery. To offer no elegiac stanzas for Milton Carswell, no tragic threnody for his wife. No. To offer instead a brilliant definition of the human predicament, and in no other way but to thrust himself into it, like a scientist like Haldane, who injected himself first with his serums because he who could understand the results must be the first to venture.

Who was my father now from whom he had been on Chelsea Street in Amherst, on autumn afternoons when his students and their parents walked through the dry, scuttering leaves toward their pleasant, sedate suppers in Little Lord Jeff, dining upon their expectations for their sons, inebriant with dreams?

He was a man intent beyond our imagining to break off from the safety of the past, of heritage and tradition as it had made him, and then to build something else, creating a new ethic as he went along through life now for the first time. In our travels whenever he would stop long enough for us to settle for a moment, as he would talk to a customer or a man in a lumberyard or to anyone at all—for he could not do other than talk now—endlessly, he would slip into the twang or drawl or nasality of the region, adapt in his own speech the local patois. Wherever we were he would assume the shape of his condition—the squint of a sailor's sun-blazed eyes, the slight stoop and lean of mountain men, the bowed waddle of the rancher, the narrow hunch of city people. He resisted nothing. And that was his giddy pleasure now—to bend to every wind, be etched by circumstance like water running sharply in a canyon, and to come again and again to the same conclusion, that we were all beyond the perceived arrangements of philosophy or science and, above all, the language of the poets. It was a truth he read in everything.

But there was contradiction enough so that, triumphant and braying about the failure of old visions as he was now, I still sensed in him the other man I had known, and for a time I even expected him, that vestigial self, to come forth at last, to step out of this new man prancing about upon this stage he had turned our lives into, and to take us both back to where we had started. But he never did.

Still, it was as if he had not altogether rid himself of his old burden as he supposed he had, but had instead undergone a terrific compression in which all the atoms of ancient compassion had coalesced into a core too small to see but of enormous density, a core of old faiths hot and molten but trapped.

At least that is how I interpret the incidents in which poetry occasionally seemed to matter to him again in the old way, as in Montana once, near the town of Riley, at that perfect gradient where the prairie slips off from the Rockies and fits down as neatly as a plowed field about the Missouri River as it slowly turns southward. We had made camp for the night, were braced against the cold of prairie nights, and now was the good time for me, the best time, the two of us, fed and nearly drowsing, between jobs, nothing but now.

In the dark the river flung itself by us not far away. Morning and afternoon we had fished in it, but mainly in the rich, glossy tributaries where the speckled trout leaped endlessly. The fire sank. He put his hand upon my head and then suddenly sang out like a benediction across the grasses hissing in the wind and against the mountains.

When I have seen by Time's fell hand defaced
The rich proud cost of outworn buried age;
When sometime lofty towers I see down-razed
And brass eternal slave to mortal rage;
When I have seen the hungry ocean gain
Advantage on the kingdom of the shore,
And the firm soil win of the watery main,
Increasing store with loss and loss with store;
When I have seen such interchange of state,
Or state itself confounded to decay;
Ruin hath taught me thus to ruminate,
That Time will come and take my love away.

He stood up quickly and shouted now again,

That Time will come and take my love away.

And again, quietly, a mutter.

That Time will come and take my love away.
This thought is as a death, which cannot choose
But weep to have that which it fears to lose.

Oh, those were the marvelous times when we touched each other across my mother's death, for in no other way could we speak of it, in all those years down all those roads. But in the nights like Montana I knew him best, and understood best, in my child's way, the cost of his strange renunciation, the price of his disdain for all our past.

My mother's death did not cause in me pain in the ordinary sense; rather, the pain of loss, of absence, a missing. I did not miss *her*; I missed what my life had felt like when she had been there to ravel me up in her sweep and gaiety. But it was into that emptiness that he rushed. Wherever I turned he was there, filling me up. My days were full of jewels flung about me like largess, gifts ceaselessly bestowed by this Prince who knew nothing any longer of boundaries. No more. I went his way with him into freedom and healed, bathed in the torrent that he had become until I grew strong in it myself and swam along with him, free as he would have me, as he wanted me to be. Only at those times when the poetry came over him did I remember that there had even been another way than this. And why we were here.

And in the Mojave, where the desert stars glinted and spangled like ice-coated trees in morning sun, I listened to the grains of sand knocked loose by the hunting spiders crashing about like boulders. All around I listened to the open death of creatures, quick and graceful, the sidewinder stalking the waiting mouse, the owl dropping down on the snake, green-eyed coyotes ranging wide of us. Then I heard him, softly now, in the old voice from long ago, to himself, to the night, to the immensity of the desert in that night, as if in the center of galaxies,

> Meanwhile, the mind from pleasure less,
> Withdraws into its happiness:
> The mind, that ocean where each kind
> Does straight its own resemblance find;
> Yet it creates, transcending these,
> Far other worlds, and other seas;
> Annihilating all that's made
> To a green thought in a green shade.

And down I dove.

IV

But who was I now from whom I had been? For if he had departed in limitless flight, an Icarus contriving through outer darknesses, had I willingly flown too? Or had I been drawn with him, inevitably, like a satellite, a moon lit brilliantly by his urgent but reflected light, secure in his gravity, fixed by his great mass, even if bound?

Not that I thought such things; not then, of course, or not that way. But later, when I came to be taught by others that dreams were metaphors of our interior terrains, I could never accept that idea so easily, for my dreams in those years seemed exactly like my life—intensely detailed, sharp and pungent and spikey with substance—and as fleeting.

Only along a thin line did my dreams and my life run together like the brown, scudding foam of a tide rising or falling in fractions of inches across a beach. There is the sea and there is the sand, but at some instant, at some point, the sea and the sand mix into something different from either; when exactly, or where, can never be told. So at times did my waking life and my dreams bond in a fluttery-edged mantle, and then I would dream clear and precise vistas that I had never seen, though I constructed them out of all my days, or else I passed awake through colossal events without remark or memory.

But on either side of that line I was never disoriented. I never confused which was the dream, or the reality, or the insubstantiality between. I could always tell which was the dream because it was shaped, hard and firm with angles and curves, posts and lintels and arches that met and bore up the feeling, the *condition*, of structure. My dreams were as rigid as my life was not—tight with streets and fences, gardens planted and ripening, a sense of *place* elegant with design, design as pervasive as a perfume. And I could tell my dreams from my waking life because in my dreams my father was never there.

Only once and only for an instant did I stumble, trip upon a dream that had come true.

For three days we had worked at installing irrigation pipes and getting the pumps to pull the water through them smoothly across the flat fields of Amiston, about fifty miles northwest of Houston. Amiston is gone now, become a school district and a zip code of Houston's suburbs, and the fields we worked in—cotton making a last stand in this part of Texas—are all paved. But then we yanked countless lengths of the light aluminum tubing into place and snapped them together with special water-tight fittings. The aluminum would quickly draw the heat of the sun and build it up, so that even through the heavy work gloves the work was hot and uncomfortable. My father had found the job at the gas stop he had made outside of Amiston. A question or two, a sense of the season's necessities, and directions were all he needed.

We showed up at Kurt Doachmann's house at dawn. I did not see the house then; I was still in the camper, hanging onto a little more sleep as best I could, like a sailor tight in his bunk, swinging through a storm. I could tell where I was in the world through the motion of the truck—highways, farms, cities; asphalt, concrete, or dirt. After thirty minutes while my father negotiated, we started off, more roughly than before, into the farm proper, riding the tractor ruts like rails.

For three days we stayed out at the farthest edge of Doachmann's land, working. Besides my father and me, there were two men whom Doachmann would bring out in the morning and pick up at night. Doachmann himself would drive the truck with the irrigation pipes, timing it so that he arrived with a new load just as we clamped down on the last pipe of the last load and before we could stop for a rest. He didn't care if we rested; all he wanted was his work done. He knew how many pipes he needed to string together each day, and that was what he brought us. His years of experience had taught him how to pace his help.

At the end of that third day Doachmann had trouble with some switches in the pumps. He could not fill his pipes, his fields. But my father worked out the problem cleverly, saving Doachmann a long trip for a replacement and the cost of an electric circuit and harness that would have cost dearly. After Doachmann had taken the other two men away, he came back and paid. We were cleaned up by then, sitting by the camper finishing supper in failing light. Doachmann sat down with us and took out a bottle of whiskey which he offered to my father, a drink which he took straight.

Doachmann liked my father's style. No cotton to dry up in a week of hot wind blowing at the wrong time through the young shoots like a devil's breath. No red dust to wash out of your clothing three times a day, to hose off your car, off your house. No watching the perfect, unblemished sun go down night after night, pulling you into a merciless, leathery bankruptcy. And if there was irrigation now, so there were the pumps that failed, the rising cost of the aluminum tubing, the water table dropping lower each year as farmers and towns and Houston sucked harder at the earth. There was the price of cotton falling to its knees beneath the pummeling of the cotton from Ghana, from Mozambique, from every goddamn place on earth where it always rained enough and the dirt was rich and new.

They had a couple of drinks, maybe more, when Doachmann said, "You. Now you go wherever you need to be. That's fine. Oh that's fine." My father did not answer. It was the kind of statement that he could enjoy, play with, make mean everything or nothing. "I know this oil rig off toward Abilene," Doachmann went on. "Maybe three hundred miles. Joseph Luft. One well, one man, all alone running the whole thing. You'd like to know Joseph Luft. He'd like to know you. He'd pay you, too. For what he needs fixed and done." Doachmann laughed. "He needs it all fixed. Everything. He'd pay you good." He took another drink. But he was not getting drunk. If anything, he was clearer. "I'll take you there. I'll go with you. In a week you could do it. Make more in a week than in a month of this." He meant the irrigation pipes. "It's nothing to be missed, I tell you. A rig like that. One man. Jesus." He slapped his leg. "We'll leave the boy with my wife and family down at the house." He stopped to think a minute, as if considering from my father's point of view. "It's a good family," he said. "They'll take fine care of him." Then, "I'm a good man," he said to my father. "There's nothing *funny* about this. It's just . . . a chance," he said.

But my father understood well enough how other men looked up from their patterns at his truck and saw the Norseman's prow, the trapper's snowshoe track, heard voyageurs singing over the boiling of the rapids. "What do you think?" he asked me. It came at me too quickly to think. I had not been apart from him for years, not even for a single night. Only in my dreams.

"Sure," I said before I could think of anything.

In the morning, when he left me at Doachmann's house and took Doachmann for his ride to Joseph Luft's one-man oil rig, I looked about and found my dream ringing hard as fact.

Doachmann's house was long and low in the prairie style, a

ranch house true enough, but made of bricks that were red and yellow and black and green that repeated themselves. On all sides of the house huge lawns banked away so that the house sat announced like a centered object with flagstone walkways (where had the flagstones come from?) leading down from the house through the lawns. The house was bordered with plantings, Texas things, century plants and flowering sage; desert things, spineless cactus and miniature yucca; but evergreens too, and rhododendrons heavily budded and nearly opened, so that it was all clearly an arrangement, an artifice brazenly unnatural, a studied act of imagination, of will as dependent upon human constancy as Doachmann's acres of cotton. The outbuildings for the farm were far down the road away from the house, but even from where I stood and in the early light I could tell that they had been placed by plans, fenced about, painted where they were not made of metal or plastic. Across from the house an orchard of peach trees covered all I could see in files and ranks.

Inside, the house was like the land around it, like my dream. It was like houses I had seen in magazines, everything where it belonged and never people in the way to mar it.

Mrs. Doachmann asked me if I would like to take a shower. From the center entrance to the house she turned me left and walked to the very end, through a dining room and then a large family room to my room with my own bath. She explained where whatever I needed was. There was even an intercom so that if I wanted something I would not have to shout or walk the length, or half the length, of the house. She left me. Breakfast would be waiting.

In the shower I luxuriated. We kept clean enough on the road, but not much more than that, and we never lived in places with fixtures like this. I stayed a long time in the hot steaming water, then dressed, slicked up with what I had, and opened my door. (A door!)

At breakfast Mrs. Doachmann, tall and friendly, Western lean, fed me pancakes and strips of steak, coffee, dishes of fresh fruits.

I met Susan, the Doachmann's ten-year-old daughter, bright and friendly with her few questions, and then gone.

Madeline came into the breakfast nook off the kitchen as I was finishing, golden, yawning, in her bathrobe. Older than I by a year or two. Or ten or twenty. What could I tell of girls or women in bathrobes, pink and swollen from sleep? Her mother scolded her for sleeping so late, for not being dressed before breakfast, for family things she had not attended to. She did not listen. I do not think she even heard. She was watching me. I found my second peach hard to swallow.

"You live in that?" she said, the first thing she said to me despite her mother's introduction. She meant the truck. They had all been told about their guest and his father.

"Yes."

"All the time?"

"Yes. I mean we sleep outside it sometimes. Sometimes we stay in a hotel or a motel. Cabins. But that's it."

"That's your home?"

"Yes."

"You wait," she said, and left. I sat around and talked a little with Mrs. Doachmann about nothing, about cotton and irrigation pipes, new ways to deal with weevils. And about her plans for me, too. All the entertainments she had arranged. There would be a day in Houston and another day beyond Houston to Galveston, some fishing there perhaps. On Saturday night a church social. She went on quickly with her list. Madeline came back, dressed in her jeans and light sweater over a thin shirt with the collar out, her hair still loose as from sleep and down her back. She could have been from anywhere, but she was not; she was a golden girl here in the Golden West.

"Come on," she said, and I had to scramble to follow her.

"Madeline," her mother called after her. "Madeline." She did not turn back.

She drove the car well, easily and relaxed. My father always drove with his own energy, as if he were making the truck go, making it bend and turn, willing it up mountains, or to stop.

But Madeline drove as easily as if she were walking, not dangerously inattentive, but disinterested.

We drove all day. She wanted to know where I had been. Had I actually seen the Rockies? New York City? Boston? The Atlantic Ocean? The Pacific? Yes I said, again and again, but that was not enough for Madeline, not nearly enough. She wanted the details, the taste of these places, the feel and tang of different air, new light. I could not say it, but she could. She would examine me, cross-examine me.

"Well, was the air *thick*? I mean was it sticky? I read that salt air gets into things, and the salt is always damp. Was it like that? Was it clammy sleeping in the truck?"

"Yes," I could say to her pictures and then add to them, go on where she led me.

And there was no end. She would circle back, actually drive back over roads that even in this one day I was beginning to recognize, but circle back too to my travels, to Montana again, Chicago, Maine, Niagara Falls.

The next day we went to Houston. Mrs. Doachmann, Susan, Madeline, me. Madeline and I sat in back while Mrs. Doachmann drove about like a tour guide. But there was little to see in Houston then, except that it was growing. It was the growing that she pointed out, that we looked at, sites and buildings going up. At the San Jacinto Memorial, in the small park, we had an illegal picnic lunch, eating it off the tailgate of the station wagon. Madeline hardly spoke to me, or to anyone at all. None of us spoke except Mrs. Doachmann, obligatory and dutiful, hostess to guest, and so back to Amiston and a late, quiet supper and early to bed. I was used to that.

I do not know when, but I woke to a soft, persistent buzzing. I sat up and finally saw off by the bed the flickering red light. The intercom. I was being called. I picked it up. It was Madeline from the far end of the house.

"Wasn't that terrible today? How did you stand it? You've got patience. You know why you've got patience?" I waited. "I *said*, 'Do you know why you've got patience'?"

"No," I said.

"It's because you know you'll be moving on. Whatever happens one day is not going to happen to you the next."

It was her revelation, and I could tell through the intercom as much as if I had my hand on hers that it was an important revelation, thrilling, something she had thought around but never till me come sharply to, though it was simple enough to see. "*You* are never going to *have* to see Houston again, but *I* will. I may have to see it *forever.*"

The thought of touching her hand crushed me. I lost my breath. She spoke on, like yesterday, asking but answering now more and more her own questions, her own necessities, spilling out places I had not been to, describing them as clearly as if she had. Just like my dreams. But I could hardly breathe. Yesterday came back. I saw her now as I had not then, had not allowed myself then, this golden girl (was she beautiful? lovely?) sitting where my father always had.

She went on for possibly an hour. Then "Good night," she said quickly, and hung up. I slept badly, tossing about upon her voice, twisting myself into what she was making of me, and arranging too my own construction of Madeline, golden, blue-jeaned, her sweater drawing slightly back across her chest that I dared to look at now, though not yesterday.

The days followed, the week swept by; Galveston, roads, farms, villages, an interesting swamp, a state park. Sometimes I even took to fixing things about the house and barns. Madeline was constantly by me. If Susan came by, she was driven off. If Mrs. Doachmann watched us, I did not know. I suppose she knew Madeline well enough and worried more for me than for her daughter. Or perhaps she knew her daughter's hunger, maybe her own hunger, and let her roam like a young mare in high fresh grass.

My hunger was coalescing, though I could not give it a name. Simply, I wanted Madeline nearby. But if I imagined more, then I imagined it along my nerve ends, in my lymphatic system, in the corridors of my youth and strength and maleness. And she went on as ever. Now she would bring a map to me and have me trace the roads we had driven, and when my finger would take her to places we had been for which there were no roads on her map, she would whoop with joy. There would be something left for her.

After the church social I lay in my bed. The intercom buzzed as I knew it would, as it had each night since Houston.

"It's me. I'll be down in an hour when they're all asleep."

"What?" I said, loudly. "Wait." But she had hung up. I got out of bed and thought to get dressed. I thought to call her, but I did not know how, feared I would ring Mrs. Doachmann instead, who would understand and prepare, stop her daughter, tell her husband. Tell my father. What was going on? What was going to go on?

In an hour she opened my door without a sound. Even in the darkness of the room I could tell her clearly. She was in her pajamas, shortie pajamas. I knew their name, things girls wore in magazines to give us pain.

She sat on the bed, her leg against mine, though I was under the covers. I wanted her to go away and I wanted her to stay. I wanted her to go away and to come back in a dream. I would know her then, understand everything and be safe as I was always safe in my dreams. But Madeline was here, no dream, and would not be leaving soon, I knew.

"Don't you ever go to school?" she asked.

"No. My father teaches me everything. He knows everything." She and Susan were on their spring vacation this week. Monday she would go back. She hated it, she said. She talked on. In a normal voice, no whisper.

She got under the covers with me. It was not a friendship, but it was not less, either. She needed to come closer to me. No, not me. Not that way; for surely there must have been other boys, men, indeed, who had held her fumingly in their bodies in her shortie pajamas. But she needed to enter me, to go through me into the bold hope and expectations of the whirlwind we all hope to ride, when we are young like Madeline perhaps, living in a ranch house on a green mound in the middle of a thousand acres of cotton row on row. I was the luck that would break her loose, the proof positive that the oceans were there, the mountains, that the world was round, that there were chances everywhere, risks.

In the morning my father would return. Already I thought he might be rising, waking Mr. Doachmann out of my bed as I was waking in his, raising Doachmann to bring him back to his solid victory over life. I wanted my father to return quickly. I floated a moment over Madeline's smell and believed for that moment in the relief that flooded me as I listened and thought I heard the tires of the truck crunch through the gravel at the edge of the prism-sharp lawns. But in the next second he was the clank of intrusion. He had entered my dream at last. Or was this the dream? The dream of fact faltering in the reality of fantasy, as the strict designs blurred into the softening amorphous drowning billowing clouds.

V

In Atlantic City we struck a special lode, a rich ore that assayed out beyond our reasonable need, but an ore mixed with a rubble heavy and intractable. It was a city that needed everything to be done with none to do it, a place to which no one paid *old* attention, so that everything was made badly and did not last, but melted down slowly instead in the leeching salt wind off the sea, melted like the sand castles children built by the sea's edges.

I was nearly sixteen when we came to this place, by now an expert of sorts in figuring new terrains, and I was growing up roughly carved and based upon instincts, the response of quick survivors. I had learned to stick my nose in the air, to check perimeters and circle twice before sitting down. Not so my father. As I grew wary in life, he grew less so, more insistent than ever on flinging out beyond the old meridians by which he had once charted his existence, more compelled than ever to discover that shapelessness which nothing—no one, no poet—could describe.

In Atlantic City he found a place nearly equal to his own distention, a city collapsing and rising with each tide, each season, each warm and sunny day. It was a terrific democracy, classless not in the traditional sense of rich or poor, but in the uniformity of its unflinching vision of a mercantile reality where only price gave truth its substance, in the city's willingness to subsume all in its meretricious pursuit of something called the tourist. And by that I do not mean the money of the tourist alone, but something more, some atavistic challenge like the hunt, predator and prey. For there was no good will in any transaction, no responsibility, however slight, between buyer and seller, as there might have been in the hometown that the tourist came from, where both buyer and seller would have to face each other the next day, and the next. Here, in the transient continuum of summer, every sale was the first and last, every deal final and for good. There was no tomorrow. Tomorrow it might rain.

My father reveled. And settled down. For the first time in our journeying we rented at length. A small private apartment in the house of Grace Franklin. 38 North Texas Avenue.

Grace Franklin was a black woman, possibly fifty, though I could not tell certainly. We had driven through the streets those first days incredulous at the opportunities for work, the entire city hanging awry. But when he stopped to make his offer, again and again he was refused. For the first time our system did not work, not at all—it failed so completely in fact that one might have put a construction upon it, or conjured up sinister explanations. But the more he was refused work, the more excited he became.

"We're into something here, I tell you," he exulted. "Maybe this is it." I did not ask him what. "I can feel it. This place—it's the beginning and/or end of things. Maybe this is where the ideas all start, or where they all come to end. Like an elephant's graveyard. Oh baby," he punched my arm. "We're going to know something after *this.*" And then we were on North Texas Avenue, cruising slowly, noting the peeling paint, the canted stair railings, the cracked sidewalks, the torn screening, dishabille poised on the edge of something worse. Only Grace Franklin's house was firm. *Apartment For Rent.* "That's for us," he said, and in half an hour we were unloading the truck and making small plans for the first time in four years.

That evening Grace Franklin fed us on flounder that she had caught out of the back bay, not more than five or six blocks from her house. "Fishing is what I do best," she said. "Crabs too. I hardly can go two days without my fishing. You get settled in, I'll take you," she said to me. "I've got a boat."

My father asked her why nothing got fixed in this city, why so much looked to need repair.

"People fix it at the last minute. Just before it gets too bad. You've got to get the rhythm. This is a tourist town. Fourth of July, Labor Day. It don't feel like you're going to *stay* long enough to need fixing. You stay here all your life, you still don't think you're home."

"And you? You fix."

"Me? Oh, I don't know."

Grace Franklin did take me fishing in the bountiful bay, showed me how to run a skiff through a tidal, chopping sea and how to find my way through the labyrinth of low marsh grass hammocks, how to stir flounder up on the bottom with a long stick, where the snapping bluefish drove the smaller fish up to spatter across the water like heavy rain, and where the deep striped bass would cruise into the bay through channels feeding on the tide. I had never known the sea, but Grace Franklin taught it to me, a good knowledge I could hammer down like a spike in my shifting life.

And my father ranged about. He had gotten his first work from a friend of Grace's, repairing the boardwalk, prying out the damaged and splintered white cedar planks and nailing in new ones.

From working on the boardwalk he slowly found other things, mostly small businesses preparing for the summer coming on quickly now, counters and racks that needed repairing, storefronts hammered together for one more season, lights rewired. The labor was quick and easy; the problems were not great. And now with an address, a place to be called, he did not need to search about for work. He could have set up in that city for good, stayed forever, sunk down roots into the sand like the starved sand grasses, the green brier, the beach plum and blue vetch, the arbor vitae. But it was not permanence he sought, not at all; he did not believe in permanence. And it was not the work, there or elsewhere, that he had ever come this far for. His only concern now, as ever, was to hammer the golden illusions of the Western world into leaf so airy thin that translucent light could pass through it and gather in it and grow warm and finally burst into incinerating flame, a puff of golden smoke. In Atlantic City he worked at that.

"To the illusionists there are no illusions," he would announce, his blue work shirt already stiff from his day's sweat. "These people are fantastic, I'm telling you. They see life steady, and they see it whole."

He would return home to us, to Grace Franklin and me, with his tales, excited, exuberant, fulfilled. More and more Grace Franklin would cook for us chowders and fillets of various fish and crab cakes, and clams in every way. And at her table or ours, he would regale us.

"They've got a diving horse up here. Listen to this. Out on Steel Pier. A girl rides this horse up a ramp to a platform, oh, maybe twenty-five feet. That's all. It jumps. A belly whopper. That's it. Splash. Think. People have *arranged* that. Effort, money, skill, struggle. I mean, what does it take to get a horse to do that? The future. Kids getting sent to college. Retirement plans. It all depends on this horse jumping into the water. It all depends upon people making a horse do that and on people who want to see it."

Drinking beer, cracking cold hard-shell crabs late into the night, laughing, telling the stories we had packed into our baggage through our travels, and what he was gathering now, he moved further out, beyond his simpler earlier attacks upon theories and principles, upon writing itself, the poets. Now he was into a purer progression, into the thinner regions of Cause, approaching Cause like a knight come to the Chapel Randomness where there was neither right nor wrong, only peril, perhaps, or at last the grail he sought, full to the brim with an elixir of perfect contempt. He was going after the connections now, directly scouring off the age-old patina of causality that had bound together over the centuries the molecules and atoms of Chaos. Let Chaos come again.

"You know what I did today? I built artist's easels for this guy on the boardwalk, Sam Euwell, the World's Fastest Portrait Artist, a title won in open competition at the 1939 World's Fair, New York. I built ten new easels and repaired five old ones for the portrait artists that work for him in the summer."

He told us about Sam Euwell, how he had won the title in 1939 (three minutes, eighteen seconds). There were five heats, eight artists in each. Then the finals. And Sam won. The best time for the best likeness. He had graduated from art school in Philadelphia ten years before that, in time for the crash and the Depression. To live, all he had was his sketching of people in the summer in Atlantic City while he stood down on the beach in the sand. For quarters. For tips. For dimes. He would draw anyone who was standing by the rail above him and then give him the picture (with a caption on it: Lover Boy or Don Juan or Casanova) and wait to see if he got anything. Or if they just walked off. Crumpled the picture and threw it back down at him. That was how it went for ten years. Then he won his title in New York and opened a small place on the boardwalk and charged set rates (one dollar for profile, a dollar-fifty for front view) to the people who sat down now under lights. Then the war came and the boardwalk was closed down, and then the war was over and he opened again and prospered, hired artists, young people still in art school, grew rich.

In the winter now Sam Euwell went to Mexico, deep into it, into the middle of Yucatan to a village of three hundred people, mostly Indian, still closer to the Mayans than to this century. All winter he would paint. Quickly.

"He showed me. Dozens of things, *hundreds,*" my father marveled. "Two, three, four a day. Quick. Like he had caught this infection in 1939 in New York. Quick. A blaze of yellows, blues, reds, like he didn't have time to mix anything."

"Yes," Grace Franklin said. "That's right. Sam Euwell." And to all the rest that he would tell us she would respond. "Yes," she would say. "Amen to that. That's right. True. No doubt. There is truth in there, yes." And to his tales she would also answer with her own, extending his discoveries, wide and deep, so that by midnight or one or two o'clock they would huff and giggle together in a superb duet, a scene out of an opera, black Grace Franklin, shining and drunk, my father, spinning in a babble of allusions to all that civilized man has ever sung, spinning further out, spiraling beyond the narrowing densities in which we assume we manage to live. For Grace Franklin was already where my father wanted to be, unencumbered by questions of reason or justice or hope, out there in the fabulous amorality of life that he was striving toward, convinced by her that at least once Aristotle was correct about something: that whatever had once happened—such as Grace Franklin—was forever possible. He did not know Grace Franklin as a person with a history maybe of victories or regrets, only as someone moving easily, sweetly on the tides.

How he knew? By her language perhaps, lilting, an east shore Chesapeake lingo? By her laughter, always laughing further than what we could understand? Because she was black, by accident put outside possibilities, and therefore already schooled in the perfectly unredemptive condition in which we all lived? Whatever, *however* he knew her, she was a charm to him, a talisman richer than all her tribe, as he styled it one summer night. And the tales she told! Ah, her tales.

"Down by Brighton Avenue near to Arctic old man Marcus had a store. Some breakfast, soup for lunch. Cigarettes, newspapers. Candy. That. But he did the numbers, too, you see. A nickel for three numbers. A quarter to box them. You know? Him and his son, Herby, they lived in the back of the store. The woman she died. In the morning after those working had gone by, later, the old people, older than Marcus, would come to play numbers. Betting so there would be tomorrow, you know? A nickel to make tomorrow come. Who could tell? Now old man Marcus, he sold dream books, what you could look up a dream in for a number. But for his old people, he kept a dream book tied on a string for them for free. So one morning a old man say to the boy, Herby, sitting on a stool at the counter, he say, 'Herby, give me a dream. I got no dreams. I'm too old. You get too old, you don't dream no more. When you're young you dream all the time. So Herby, give me a dream.'

"'I got no dreams,' Herby say.

"'Come on, gimme a dream,' the old man say. Back and forth they go. Until old man Marcus say to Herby, in his ear, 'So make up a dream. What's the matter with you. It's such a big deal? Give him a dream, he'll play a number. Nickels is nickels.'

"'Orange juice,' Herby say to the old man, looking down into the orange juice he is drinking.

"The old man goes to the dream book on the string and looks up *orange juice.*

"'No orange juice,' he say. 'Only *oranges.* Is *oranges* OK, Herby?'

"'Yeah, fine. Great. *Oranges* is just as good.'

"So the old man plays his nickel on *oranges,* which is 358. And the number hits. The next morning a dozen old people are begging Herby for a dream. Everybody gets a dream.

"And do you know, one dream number, it hit again.

"On the third day people old and young are lined up outside the store to go in, get a dream, find its number and play it with old man Marcus. Business was good, never better. Nothing hits, but it was too late for that now. And in the afternoon Herby walked down Brighton Avenue across Arctic, all around, like a king, smiling to the left and to the right. Oh, you should just have seen him strut. Hey, that's Herby Marcus. He dreams numbers! Hey, Herby, gimme a dream, and here and there Herby would lean over and give a dream away for nothing. No nickel. No play at all.

"On the fourth morning there were people all the way down the block pushing and shoving and waiting for a dream. Inside the store Herby would look around and say what he saw, say it was his dream. Napkins, eggs, cigars. Outside a policeman kept order.

"On the fifth day Joe Ponzio showed up. He owned the numbers that side of the city. What was going on? What Joe Ponzio had heard was bigger than what was, but all the people waiting, that was no good. That kind of attention was bad, even with everybody paid off, cops and all.

" 'No more dreams,' he told Herby, told old man Marcus. So that was over. Joe Ponzio gave Herby a job right on the spot. Bringing in the policy, the numbers slips. And carrying back the payoff, when there was one. If. But no more dreams. And when he walks down Brighton Avenue or thereabouts, even now, no one looks at him or cares."

"Oh," my father would croon at such stories as Grace Franklin told. "Oh yes." And Grace Franklin, she would say *yes* back. They were in agreement, that was clear; but about what?

"What?" I asked her out in the skiff in the last of the darkness drifting across a feeding tide into morning. In September. Labor Day just past. The Miss America Pageant two days away. All summer I had spoken to Grace Franklin. For more than four years now I had spoken to no one but my father, and to him I mostly listened. But I spoke to Grace Franklin all summer, telling her where we had been, what we had seen and done, about Montana and St. Louis, Walla Walla and the Mojave. And about Amherst. Sometimes I spoke to her of my mother, of what I remembered about her, and how what I remembered faded in some ways but grew strangely sharper in others; but what grew sharper might not have been as it had really been, but what I had made it. Or my father, in his magnificence, had made of it. And she would say *yes* to me too. Yes to what? "What? What do you see? What does he see? You're always agreeing with each other. What is he looking at? He's always looking out at something. What is he always looking out at?"

"In one word? He's looking at what you can't say in one word. Like this. What would you call this?" She wiped her arm across the bay, the island, the pine-marked mainland, but by *this* she meant the dawn, the false dawn, it is called; before the sun rises but where there is light, or lightness, rather, but no contrast, so that though you can see objects clearly, you cannot tell accurate distances, as if the world were all a flat mosaic on a wall in a single tone, a world true but utterly untrue, and full of dangers should you try to move, to moor a boat or reach carefully over a sandbar. Birds do not fly in the false dawn. The water is still. The small sounds come from everywhere. It is a moment as sublime as it is terrifying, for to live, even for a few minutes, as thin as a dampness across space, is to come as close to death as it might be—clear, formed, exact, but nothing, nothing at all. "This is what he's looking at. Me too."

Then the sun broke out of the sea, the grayness washed off. Sound oriented. Sea birds rose from the tar-cloaked pilings. She yanked the outboard motor alive and we powered across to a sand spit between the bay and the ocean, where mackerel running south would come close to the shore in September, and where we would take them, slashing and bright, striped like blue tigers, out of the breaking waves.

Three days after the Miss America Pageant he told me we were leaving Atlantic City.

"Pageant," he said. "What a word. Pageant. Pageantry. Quote, a public spectacle illustrative of the history of a place, unquote. The pageant of history. The pageant of the Plantagenet. The Pageant of Miss America." He was standing on the porch of Grace Franklin's house, shouting out to North Texas Avenue. Then he said, raising his arms to the street, commanding it, or supplicating it:

> For God's sake let us sit upon the ground
> And tell sad stories of the death of Kings.

"Come on," he said to me, "let's pack." Then, "After such knowledge, what forgiveness, right? So let's go."

For the first time since that June in Amherst when we left the old ways for good, I did not want to go on, because even though we would have something more to remember, another alm for him to put in his packet against oblivion, now we would also have something else to forget. But by four in the afternoon, we were ready.

"Goodbye, Grace," he shouted up to her. She was on her porch; we were by the truck. "Goodbye," that was all.

"Goodbye," she said.

"Goodbye," I said.

"Goodbye."

And we drove off, first to Camden across the state and then across the Delaware River and then down through Wilmington to a campground just beyond it, arriving about nine o'clock. I said nothing from Atlantic City to there, but not him. He talked forever, pleased at our long interlude, doubly pleased that he could leave it, pull up and go on, excited to be off again to prove again in a new place by a new configuration that nothing was, but seeming made it so; that nothing *anywhere* had changed, or could.

But I was grumpy and annoyed, as if in his mad rush he had zoomed past the answer, the secret, as if he had missed the turnoff, taken the wrong path. I was weary of his misanthropic cant. I'd had enough. Maybe I needed to work out my answers for myself. At least to try on my own.

The next day we drove long and hard, down past Baltimore to Washington, heading for North Carolina, for Raleigh, whenever we got there.

"The trouble with you is you want too much order. You want everything to be perfect, just right." I had to stop him. He had been going on about mutations and chi squares and Darwinian selection and phylogenetic profiles, about how powerful new evidence was mounting to show that change in living forms was not, as had been long accepted, simply the result of survival pressures: that life forms changed nearly as much for no reason as for one. He was explaining once more how it was our picture of things that was ordered, but not what we were looking at; how we embraced the picture, worshiped it, and made it stand in place of what we truly had. At my complaint he ignited.

"Yes yes yes yes. *Order* is not comparative."

"What does that mean?" I tried to sound truculent, to douse him with the cold matter of disinterest; but I was his son, imprinted by him like soft gold under his seal and hammer, and I rose to him like bait.

"It means that you can't have *more* order or *partial* order, the same way you can't have a fuller pail of water. It is either full or something else. You have either got order or something else. Well, we've got something else, and we don't want it, so we spend our lives working out rationales. Orders. One for you and one for me and one for him, for it, for them. This war, that betrayal, the collapse of a star, the movement of continents, hunger, pestilence, triumphs and Waterloo. We make it all make sense. And Law, oh yes, Law is everywhere. And when you run out of explanations, you drop to your knees and kiss God's ass. Or you turn fascist. Or go mad. Or blur it in alcohol."

"How can you say that?" I shouted at him. "How can you just *say* that?"

"Because I've read the poets, sweetheart. I've read it all from then to now and it's all the same, whatever the shape."

"So what?" I said. "What's it to you?"

"It's all I've got to give you."

"*Give me? Give me what? What are you talking about?*"

"This," he said.

But if by *this* he meant my life just then, I did not want it. I had had enough of riot; like other men (for I was becoming one), I wanted what I could dream of having *even if* I could not have it, so I had not yet learned from him what he would have me know. Or I had not accepted it. His gift. Yet.

"I want to go to Harrisburg. I want to live with Aunt Karen. For a while." I bit back tears. I did not want to leave him. Ever. And I did.

In twenty yards he turned right because there was a road there that went west instead of south toward Raleigh, And when he could he turned north, threading his way across and through the Cumberlands toward Harrisburg.

"It's a good idea," he said. If he was hurt, I could not tell, though I doubt that he was. "I'll call Aunt Karen at the next gas stop. Listen, Harrisburg's got some fun in it. And girls. You should be hanging around girls by now. Playing some baseball maybe." And by the Pennsylvania and Maryland border, the old Mason-Dixon Line, he was as ebullient as if he were the one who was off on this adventure, this new turn, this possibility. This demonstration.

He stayed with us in Harrisburg for two days, helping make the arrangements, though there was little to do. His sister, Karen, had offered to take me time and again. She had room. He busied himself with her storm windows, old-fashioned green wood-framed windows. He puttered around. For two nights at supper with his sister and her husband, Hank, he seemed to be the professor again, the man they remembered, quiet though spirited, cogent, precise, polished, urbane. As if he had simply put on an old jacket from the past, a little tighter here and there, but a comfortable fit still. As if we had not traveled to the moon. As if my mother had not careened away.

On the third morning he went with me to the high school I would attend, to explain why I had no record of schooling for four years and to convince them that I was educated sufficiently for their task of going on with me. Aunt Karen came, too. And in an hour and a half it had worked out well enough.

Back at the house we said goodbye. We spared each other as much as we could.

"I'll call," he said. "I'll be around."

"Sure," I said. "I'll want to see you."

Then he got into the truck and drove off, and not till later in the day did I despair, for even then I knew that I had not bought order, only decorum, the simulacrum of order, and that they were not the same, and he was right. That the answer—to what question?—was not here. He had driven off with the answer, whatever it was or could be. Out there where each morning began uncertain of its conclusion, just the way it was.

School, acquaintances, a good bed, studies, games, TV, explicit meals, my good Aunt Karen and Uncle Hank—I lasted ten days and then went after him.

He would turn back down to Raleigh, he had told us. I would find him. I was road wise, even at sixteen. And I had his pattern in me. And now his great faith in uncertainty, which could cut both ways: my odds were *always* even. I would find him because I could find *anything* just as likely as not. And if the road from Corinth was the road to Thebes, as he had taught me, then who was I to venture less?

Thumbing sometimes, busing mostly, I got to Raleigh in under two days and started to sort out the city, figuring it out as we had over and over, looking for the neighborhoods old enough to need work and yet not so well off that a bargain could not be struck. I asked around for him. He had been here. And there. Five days ago.

I looked for two more days. Learned Raleigh quickly. Stayed in a motel because I could tell the manager and clerks how my father was going to meet me and because I could talk to them so that they were not suspicious or alarmed, because I had been here before, everywhere before.

My money was nearly gone. But I was not frightened. He had taught me: nothing *must* happen if *anything* might. And on the third day I found him on Vickers Street, the red truck parked in front of a house he was mending. I heard him hammer. I got into the truck and waited. Two hours. When he came out and saw me, "Well," he said. "Well." And then, "Well, I'll be damned." I took him in my arms and kissed him. Then we drove off.

"What's in Georgia?" he said. "Pick something."

And drove on for five more years into episodes. But I could not match him, could not fly with him into the nether regions where he beat like a great winged creature, though when at last I did leave him to go my way, I left as rich as any princeling ever did.

Now I have a wife and children, and I have told them tales. So when there are days when I take long, restless drives alone, read maps, remember places, my wife understands. As if no place is mine.

And only my father, bold artificer, great wanderer, only he is home.

The Garden

He hammered the sharp, stinging sound into the thick, wooded hills that cupped his land in a bowl, driving the large #16 common nails into the new joists and rafters and studs and then into this terrain. He meant to stay. He had taken the inheritance and had put it down, like a gambler, perhaps, but not like a fool: there had been method, if not system. And his father would have approved. It was not the taking of chances that got you into trouble, it was the bad odds. So he had played it safe enough. He had learned what he needed in Rhode Island and then in Sweden, and now, with what was left of the money, he had bought this place and the tools and machinery for his work, and the important wood. From now on whatever happened was up to him.

He drove the nails with the heavy framing hammer. With each two-pound blow the nail sang higher, as the length of the steel shortened into the lumber: first a percussive thud and then three rising notes, thin and vibrant as harmonics on an E string. The weather had been good for building, had rained little. This extension to the rickety house would be finished by the weekend; not the casements or insulation and wiring, or the painting and trim, but the framing and sheathing and siding. He could take his time with the rest and with fixing the old house itself. He had all the summer that was coming after this good spring. And more. But by Sunday he could set up his tools and machines and benches in the extension, and then begin to think of the cabinets and chests and tables he would build out of the planks of pearwood and beech and cherry that he had stored in the air under tarpaulins. But now he kept his mind to this task, saving the promise of the cabinets and tables as once he had saved the promises of dessert.

He turned the last joist on edge and tugged it a fraction until it dropped into place, the notches he had cut in the two-by-six sliding down firmly and exactly. He sighed with small pleasure as the pieces of wood melded. Heavy rafters or dovetail joints along the edges of elegant boxes, it was the same to him. He handled all wood the same way. He spiked the rafter down at either end and in the middle across the central beam. He stood up. This was done. He would stretch, go down, drink some coffee, and then begin to cover the roof with the plyscore. He looked around at the rimming hills and picked out birch and maple and white oak that he would take down someday, to be sawed into material by a mill. And the air was still dry. It would not rain. It might not rain for a week.

The battered Volkswagen popped and shuddered its way up his hill, kicking stones out of the loosened gravel road, the sound of the car rolling around more and more quickly as it came closer until it was directly down from him, next to his truck in the rough driveway. It stopped. The last of its banging waved back over the hills. She got out of the car.

"I'm Jane Friant," she shouted to him and then ducked back into the car and hauled out a paper shopping bag, *Pricechoppers* printed on both sides of it. She picked her way through the flotsam of the building site. "I'm Jane Friant," she said next to him, quietly. "I live over there." She pointed widely to the entire east, to the horizon, to the Green Mountains of Vermont. But then, more precisely, "On Christie Road. I live about five miles down. A small house, a few acres, a loaf of bread, a jug of wine. And a view. Hi." She put out her hand. They shook. "I heard you were here, but I've been traveling a little and working a lot. And the gardening this time of year takes what's left and more. I would have come sooner." She looked around. "Where's *your* garden?"

"No garden."

"No garden? But what are you going to talk about?" She

laughed, thrush-like, watery and quavering. "Whenever we get together, that's what we all talk about, our gardens. Whose peas have come in, how heavy the Japanese beetles are this year, what to do about slugs, blossom-end rot in the tomatoes, strategies to foil the woodchucks. I think you should put in a garden in self-defense. Oh, here." She handed over the shopping bag. "Welcome."

"How about some coffee?" he asked, taking the bag.

"Sure." She followed him toward his house. "Can we have the coffee in the new room? I love, it, the skeleton of a house, where you can see how it all works. There are very few things you can see that way, clearly, all at once, what makes it all work. It's a shame you have to cover it up."

On chairs that he brought out of the house they sat under the open rafters. She had brought him homebaked bread and jars of jelly, jam, and preserves, all her own. They ate the bread and jelly and drank the boiled coffee that he had quickly made. She drank the coffee and winced.

"This coffee is awful. The bread and jelly are terrific but the coffee is awful." She made her thrush-laugh. She looked about at the strict intelligence of the walls of studs with the headers set for the windows, the wide sills, the tripled two-by-fours that made up the corner columns.

"I guess you don't want more?" He held the camping pot up by its long bail, offering.

"Oh well, why not. Half a cup." He poured. She looked into the cup. He watched her face. Her skin was very smooth. Even in the April chill, her skin did not tighten across her bones.

Then she said, "I feel like something in a *New Yorker* ad." With her hands she placed the caption for him in the air. "Frame up." She started to write the copy, then stopped. "Guess what the ad is selling."

He shrugged. "The house?" He did not read the *New Yorker.*

"Oh no, the ad never sells what it first seems to be about. Go ahead, guess again." She sipped the coffee and puckered. Then, "Oh," like a gasp. "Look."

She pointed up with her finger, but did not raise her arm. "The hawks. Red-tails. He's courting her." They looked up. One hawk swung slowly up and up, in infinitely small increments but in a widening gyre. It did not appear to be rising. All around that hawk the other hawk, the male, barreled and looped, racing unimaginably high and then dropping like a diver tucked tightly into himself, hurtling past her and then in an instant braking and pulling up before her, throwing wide his wings, the pinions still streaming, in a massive display. Then he would fall back and begin again to thread through her slow, tightly banked spiral.

They looked up through the rafters, so they could only see the hawks slatted, chopped as in a strobe effect or like stop-action photos put on film run quickly. The hawks were here and then here and then here.

"'The achieve of, the mastery of the thing,'" she quoted. He chewed her bread slowly. "Hopkins?" she offered. The hawks had sailed away.

She was Jane Friant. She lived on Christie Road and took care of herself and was trying to succeed as a writer of fiction here in the hills of Washington County in upstate New York, hard upon the border of southern Vermont. She had graduated from Bennington, not far from here, three years ago and had been busy ever since, writing and raising food and putting it by.

"How's it going?" he asked.

"Which, the writing or the garden?"

"Both."

"Well, I haven't missed any meals yet. But writing? How can you tell? I'm happy with what I do. I get stories published in good little literary magazines often enough to make me think I'm alive and well. I get myself invited to colleges to give readings and to be on panels. I apply for grants. I review books for twenty-five dollars and the books. I write letters to editors. I keep in touch. Is this an answer?" She reached out and put her hand over his. It was hard and calloused like his own, a laborer's hand, a field worker's hand. Was she asking him this, or only demanding his closest attention? "I'm writing well enough to suit me. I know

I'm not kidding myself. I've got a right to do this. I'm not living in a romantic fantasy. I'm working hard at what I want to do." She released him.

"Is that enough?" he asked. "For a writer, I mean? Isn't there more? I can make these chairs and sit on them and that's enough, except I need money so I'll try to sell them. But a writer can't do that, can you? You can't use a story. You can't just stop with the writing."

"No," she said. She stood up and walked about on the rough sub-flooring, as on a stage. Her work boots beat upon the flooring. She stuck her hands into the back pockets of her jeans, tightening her plaid mackinaw shirt across her flat chest. "No," she said. "You're right. A writer must have an audience. *Must!*" she shouted the word. It circled up like the hawks had. At the opening for one of the large windows that would look out to Vermont, she turned and stood like a painting in the frame. Her hair, long and black, had fallen free of whatever had held it. She hoisted herself up onto the window sill and braced herself against the jack studs that would hold the casement, wrapping her arms around them as if they were the chains of a playground swing. "And there's more, curse it. There's fame and fortune. And praise. Adulation. Immortality."

She was laughing now, shouting and laughing, telling the truth and stepping back from it too. "I'm twenty-five," she shouted to him from her window seat across the work room. She leaned forward, straining, as if she would force the sill to swing high into the room. "I've got thirty-five more years to win the Nobel Prize." She whooped and clapped her hands and tottered a little on the window sill.

"Look out," he said. He reached out his hand as if he could reach her to steady her.

"What?" she shouted over her own noise, over her own ebullience.

"Look out," he said again. "Don't fall."

"Oh no," she said. "Not me." She hopped down from the window sill and came back to him.

They finished half the bread and a good part of the jar of jelly. It was a jelly made from violets. She talked to him about where he was, what it was like here in season, where to buy things that he might need, who lived hereabouts. Then he stood up. He had half a day's work left, the roof to sheath and more. He explained that he would do the roof before the walls, so he could use the large room for storage right away. He had wood waiting for him at Hartley's in New York, rosewood and Brazilian mahogany, and there was ash and butternut that he would pick up from a friend outside Poughkeepsie. He needed the storage. He walked with her down to her car.

"Thanks a lot," he said. "Thanks for the welcome. I'm sorry I can't sit longer. We'll do this again."

"Why don't you come for supper?" it occurred to her, and she brightened to the idea. "Sure. Come on. I'll have Jaeger and Mara over. They're painters from further down the road. Come on. Start to meet the folks."

"Like this?" he said. "I stink. I haven't had a shower in a week. The hot water's not hooked up yet." But he did want to go to her supper.

"Come early. Take a shower at my place. Come at seven. I'll tell Jaeger and Mara to come at eight." She started the car and turned it around, the noise of it a conclusion. As she started to drive away, he shouted for directions.

"Christie Road," she barely shouted back as the car started to skid and twist down the driveway. "You'll see the car."

He fell. He reached to pull a sheet of the heavy three-quarter-inch plywood into square across the rafters, and the brace he had laid down to stand against snapped under him. He slid three feet down the incline of the roof and then into the house, between the rafters that he had set on sixteen-inch centers—close enough to bear the heavy snows he had been warned of, wide enough for a man to fit through. As he dropped, he fell against the jagged end of the broken brace. A large slivered end stabbed into him, a knife of wood thrusting up into the large muscle over his left shoulder blade. He landed softly, bending into the shock, taking it the way a spring compresses; then he let himself out and up like a gymnast coming off the high horse. And then he flattened himself quickly on the sub-flooring, the pain sparking in him, up through his neck and down his entire left side into his ankle.

He let the pain alone. You could not fight the pain. He closed his eyes and waited. The pain was like a sound in him, a roaring. He tried to think what the sound was, if it was a locomotive, or the wind, or a waterfall. He gave it up, letting the sound increase until it began to block itself. When the pain finally receded from the rest of his body and settled into a throb in the actual wound, he sat up slowly and reached around to touch. He could not reach the wound, only the end of the spear of wood. He took the end of the wood in his fingers and yanked it out quickly. His blood ran a little but clotted in his shirt and against his back.

He climbed back up onto his roof. He established a firmer brace, squared the four-by-eight sheet of plywood and nailed it down. And then another sheet, and the next, through the afternoon until the roof was covered. The shoulder would hurt more in the morning than it did now. The bruise would be worse than the cut. Now he hardly felt it. What he felt was the house tightening, coming into being accurately. He went about with his four-foot-long straightedge, testing the plumb of the studs and the corner columns to see if he had skewed them with the roofing, but nothing had moved. The bubble in the leveling tube floated unvaryingly between the scored lines. What he felt was a future coming into a shape. For the rest of the afternoon he worked at cutting the hole in the roof and boxing it where the metal chimney of his wood stove would emerge.

At six o'clock he stopped and came down. It was darkening. Next week daylight saving time would start again, and he would have more time to work at the end of the day. And it would be warmer. Winter had not altogether gone out of the land. There were cracks and pockets all over with ice still in them. And in the clear, cloudless high-pressure weather the night temperatures would drop far down, to two or three degrees Celsius at the least.

He rummaged in his sleeping room in the old house for clean clothes. He wrapped underwear and socks in a heavy cotton shirt, and those in a pair of clean denims. He took out of the closet a thick and intricate poncho designed and woven for him by Heldogras in Sweden.

Heldogras. He would look at her from the woodworking shop, across the courtyard. She would be working at the great loom, with the beater swinging from the overhead beam. At ten o'clock each morning, never sooner, she would turn to look for him and then wave. One day at ten o'clock she had held up the finished poncho and waved it like a flag, a signal, and then she had put it on. It fit her as well as it would fit him. He understood. He left the workshop and went over to her in the weaving studio, sawdust and wood shavings trailing after him. Heldogras's teacher had scolded him for his dust.

They left the weaving studio right then, Thursday morning, and they did not return to their classes until Monday noon.

The Konstfackskolan was fixed on the far north edge of Stockholm, just where the city begins to flutter off into the endlessness of the Swedish coniferous forests that wash unbroken into the northern snow fields. They left the Konstfackskolan and stayed together wherever the next day, the next hour, would lead them. They made no plans, needed none. By Sunday they were in Gaule, 185 kilometers from Stockholm. Heldogras had friends in Gaule, and, all of them drunk, her friends drove them back by three o'clock in the morning to his apartment, to his room in the apartment that he shared with Kurt and Bjorn. When he and Heldogras had awoken at seven, he had gotten out of bed and put on the poncho to go to the bathroom. The wool on his bare skin was like Heldogras had been—not rough at all, but surprising, a sensitivity like loving itself. Unbearable. He had taken off the poncho and gone naked past Kurt and Bjorn in the kitchen.

Peter Martin. She had contrived his name into the poncho on its inner side at the back of the neck. She said she had done that because now whenever he wore the poncho he would feel his name there and remember her. And that was true.

He put the poncho back carefully on its special hanger in the closet. From one of his duffle bags he hauled out a dark brown crew-necked elbow-patched sweater, his freshman football sweater from Brown. In Sweden he had removed the numerals from it. But, as with Heldogras's poncho, when he wore this sweater he remembered that past, too.

His history was a history of leavings. He had gone to Brown for a year—his father's school, and what would have been his father's choice for him. But Brown had been his own choice too, as much as any other. He had no argument for or against Brown. He went. It had been a satisfactory year, but it had not meant enough to him to want to return. In that year he had found the Rhode Island School of Design: the shops, the machinery, the skills, the lucidity of the purposes, the elegance of the India ink on the white scrolls—it all alerted him. He was admitted to RISD and stayed two years, increasingly centering on woodworking until the dean had called him in to talk about his "overwhelming exclusivity," the dean had called it. The dean was sympathetic and helpful. He had seen it happen often, young design students falling into love with the making itself, finding themselves as craftsmen first and maybe forever. It was a good discovery to make. Better happily now than miserably later, when it was too late to do anything about it. The dean had told him about the Konstfackskolan. He told him that it was the best of all possible places to learn his craft. His art.

He had stayed at the Konstfackskolan for two years, twenty-four continuous months with only small vacations. He could have stayed another year to complete the three-year program, but there was no more that he needed to learn. The third year would have been a year of refinement.

And it would have been a third year with Heldogras. Then he had thought that, if he had stayed with her for that year more, he would never leave her. He would either stay in Sweden or bring her back to this country. Back to what? He had thought that then. Now he did not know.

He knelt down and reached far under his bed for a pair of shoes. He hadn't worn shoes since he had sat with the lawyers and closed on the property. From then on he had worn only his usual work boots. As he reached far under for his shoes, the wound on his back split apart slightly. He had forgotten it. The chill had deepened. His sweat had caked around him in the cold, stiffened, so the wound had opened more like a break, a fracture. He had left Heldogras and he did not want to think about it.

The water streamed over him in vines and cords and ribbons. His week and the April coldness washed off and out of him. He had shaved first and now he was showering, turning the water hotter and hotter each minute or two. He remembered the sauna heat of Sweden, him and Heldogras in the sauna in the basement of her apartment house, where sometimes there would be seven or eight men and women mixed together. He had never gotten used to that. But he had learned heat. Dry or wet, he had learned the pleasure of it, the heat working through the flesh down to the bones and then into the bones themselves. The bathroom was blank with steam. The water cleaved his skull. He looked down, and around his feet the water swirled pink from his blood.

He reached around his back to feel the wound, but everything was too wet. He turned off the shower and watched as blood ran down his haunch and his leg. He moved his left arm. There was still a piece of wood in him. The heat had worked it loose enough to hurt. When he moved his arm, the bleeding quickened.

He dried off as much of himself as he could and then wrapped the towel around his waist and tucked it into itself. The blood spread in the towel. He would owe her a towel. He opened the bathroom door and called her. In the small house the bathroom was on the same floor as the kitchen. He called again. When she got to the bathroom he explained before she could be surprised.

She was very efficient. She ordered him to lie down on the floor, on the towel she placed over the rug in front of the Franklin stove with its small fire. She brought over a professional-looking box of assorted bandages and bottles, pins, tweezer, clamps, cotton gauze and other things in plastic bags. It looked like more than first aid. She sponged the wound and examined it closely. She felt around it with her fingers.

"Does this hurt?" She pinched gently.

"Haah," he arched with the pain.

"Yes. Well, the problem is that a piece of wood is lodged in there at an angle. It's got to come out. Whenever you move the wood saws away in there."

"Take it out," he said.

"Me?"

"No. The cat. Get the goddamn cat to do it." He did not like to be hurt or sick. More than discomfort, he would feel anxiety, a low-grade infection of panic seeping through him when his body did not work right.

"Listen, it's deeper in there than you think. I'd have to fish around to get at it. That would *really* hurt. And you need something to prevent infection anyway, and probably a tetanus shot. Come on. I'll take you to the hospital. We can get there in fifteen minutes. It's over in Cambridge. I'll leave a note for the Jaegers." She continued to sponge his back.

"No. Just do it. Clean wood is safe. You don't get infected."

"That's an old wives' tale. You can get infected by any unsterile . . ."

"Will you just *do* it? Will you just shut up and *do* it?" He tightened all over. He rose up a little. The pain was severe in that position. It knocked him down.

She went to work. He felt the cold tweezer like a branding iron on his skin, but that was all he felt there. What happened now was like the splinter had turned into a large spike and was driving into his heart through his lungs. He could not breathe. He squirmed and arched up. She put her knee on him and forced him flat and still.

"I've got hold of it. Don't move. Here goes." She pulled it out. He screamed and crawled forward nearly out of his loosened towel. The heat from the Franklin stove quickly warmed his exposed rump. She drew the towel back up over him. He sobbed once, a great heaving out of the rest of the trauma. She stroked his neck and with her other hand continued to sponge the wound. Then she held a large gauze pad to it.

"It's stopping," she said. "You could probably use a couple of stitches, but I have some butterfly bandages and they might work. I'll try to stop the bleeding first with surface pressure. That's the best way."

He was exhausted. The long day of work, the accident, the relaxing shower, this tension and pain. But it was more the release that had drained him. He could have held out, but he could not contain the giving in: he swept down the backwash, grew bleary and vague and thick under her hands.

"You know all about this?" he said.

"This is the country. I'm a member of the Volunteer Emergency Corps. They give you a good first-aid course. Do you want to join? We always need people." She rubbed an antiseptic salve over the wound and replaced the pressure pad. She continued to rub his neck.

He was falling asleep. His voice was drifting away from him. "Are you taking notes? Are you going to write about this?"

She was surprised. "No." Then, "Yes. But not how you think it. Did you ever hear of Trigorin, the character in Chekhov's play *The Seagull*?" She guessed that he had not. "He was always writing things down in a notebook that he carried with him. Whatever caught his eye or his ear he would write down. He would make his stories out of what he saw or heard—nothing less, but nothing more. He would never be a great writer, and he knew that about himself. He allowed life to determine beforehand what he could imagine. That makes your own life count for too much." She had stopped rubbing his neck. "You've got to be free of your own life if you're going to do something great. Do you understand?"

"No," he said, mumbling into sleep. "Just don't write about me. I wouldn't want to find myself in a story."

"Why not?" she asked him, but he was gone. She sat a few more minutes, holding the gauze pad tight to his back until she was certain that he had stopped bleeding. His breathing evened out. She put her free hand softly on his back across from the wound. He shivered through all his muscles, his entire body rippling like a horse shedding flies. She dressed the wound and went back to preparing supper.

"My god, she's killed him!" Jaeger said as soon as he came into the house, Mara behind him. The outside cold scuttled in across the floor and shook him. He rose like a diver kicking up into the air; out of his depths, he popped awake and gasped. Now the three of them stood around him. He looked at their heavy shoes.

"This is Peter Martin," Jane said. "The body down there on the floor." They all laughed, Peter too. He worked his towel tight around himself and stood up. "Peter, this is Mara and Bob Jaeger, but we call him Jaeger." They all laughed yet harder. Peter held onto his towel and shook hands with them with his free hand.

"Talk about a compromising situation," Jaeger said. "And you only met him this morning you say? I think I need a drink to handle that." He walked off to the kitchen to help himself. "And you," he said back to Peter, "you had better get dressed."

Jane had been right. Without a garden he would have to listen more than talk, but it was good listening. Their gardens were calculations, *acts* as much as necessities, arrangements with complexities and resolutions, like war or art. Jaeger was going to move his tomatoes this year to lower ground and his onions higher, where the drainage was better. The seeds for the French squash, the courgette, had arrived, and he would give Jane five of them. She gave him the address of a good and inexpensive supplier of shallot bulbs, a secret to be kept. Mara would try once again to raise celeriac to a size that made it worthwhile.

But they brought him in, talked about Washington County to him, who and what and where. And then beyond. Jaeger told them about New York, Paris. Galleries. Sales and near sales. Jaeger was fifty-five, florid, effusive, squirish in his ragged patch-pocket tweed. He had come to his small success as a painter only about five years before. After nearly thirty failed years, as simply as it had formerly been difficult, a gallery in Paris accepted some work which immediately sold well. Now he could not paint fast enough. Each year he would have a show. For thirty years he had lived on Mara's trust fund, and now this. Mara herself was a watercolorist, successful within a fifty-mile radius of their studio-home farther down on Christie Road.

"And you?" Mara asked him. He told them what there was to

tell about how he had come to settle here, and what he wanted to do with wood. He told them about RISD and the Konstfackskolan in Stockholm. He made some sketches for them of his designs. They were delighted.

"No one else around here is doing that," Jaeger said. "You should do well."

Jane's house had delighted him at once. He followed the home-made invention of it quickly, noticing the off-balanced dimensions of the rooms, the odd placements of doorways, the windows higher than usual. It was a well-built house but differently constructed, a house made by a good carpenter with a strong will who just might have been in a hurry. He asked her if she knew the house's history. It was quite small for a country house, built as it was in a time when houses were made three generations large.

The house had been built in 1868 by Frederick Whinney for his grandmother, Freda Mattheu Whinney, "'who would not live with us,'" Jane quoted. She took him to a small panel in the band of wainscoating that cinched the entire interior of the house and removed the panel. There it was neatly carved: the information and the statement. Frederick Whinney had signed his house and given his reasons or explanation. The rest was up to posterity.

Jane had made her house bright and do-daddy in authentic country style, with starched chintz curtains, old gray crocks and jugs with blue eagles on them that she still used, implements and bowls of lustrous wood oiled and burnished by decades of use, cast-iron cranks and wheels and three-legged pots and hooks and hinges and latches from the century before.

The gold-rimmed glasses she wore now fogged up slightly in the change from the cooler rooms to the hot kitchen. Her smooth skin gleamed in her own warmth, and she was rouged by her exertions as she bustled about.

When they ate it was from her larder: leeks, potatoes, onions, stewed tomatoes, brussels sprouts. Pickled cucumbers. The last of the Belgian endive from the crate of sand in the root cellar under the house, and carrots still crunchy and stiff. A few small leaves of lettuce already from the cold frame in the back yard. Her own heavy, wheaty bread. Two small roasted chickens (from a neighbor) stuffed with apples and nuts. Apple pie. Freshly ground coffee.

The Jaegers had brought the wine. Jaeger explained the fine points of what they were drinking and told excited tales of his discoveries in the back road vineyards of France, as he styled them. Now that he visited France so often, he could make and keep contacts, he said, getting in on the good things like this 1965 St. Emilion from Monbousquet that they were drinking.

"It's as good as anything from Château Cadet-Bon and half the price." He had poured for them again. And again.

Jane's house, the food, the wine, the gardens, weather, terrain and history of Washington County. Fragrant apple wood in the Franklin stove. The rising tax rate (on his land too), the new bridge over the river at Battenville (the childhood home of Susan B. Anthony), the layoffs at the paper mill in Center Falls, the good guys and the bad. Sweet. A savoring. The sweetness of this possession. This all belonged to him. Now he belonged to it. It was the first of anything that he had. He leaned into it, full. Already the wound in his back was beginning to itch, a sign of healing. He had always been quick to mend.

"Do you know what a hutch is?" Jaeger asked. "A colonial hutch? If I showed you a picture of it, could you make it? In pine?" Jaeger was a little drunk, but so was he, and he was tired too, heavy with his contentment.

"Sure," he said. "I can make anything."

"Can you make this hutch if I show you the picture?"

"Sure."

"Don't talk business at dinner," Mara said.

"OK. OK. I won't talk business. A trade. I'll talk a trade. A trade between gentlemen and artists." He turned back to Peter. "You make the hutch and I'll give you a painting. I'll pay for the materials. Deal?" He reached out his hand. Peter reached across and took it.

"Deal," he said.

He did not want to make the hutch. He did not want to make something from a picture of something that Frederick Whinney's great-grandfather might have made. And he did not want to work in pine. Anyone could work in pine. You could nearly punch pieces out of pine like the pieces in model airplane kits printed on balsa wood. He could make a pine hutch with a penknife. Even maple would have been better, but maple was dull. Hutches were dull. "How about a trunk?" he said. "How about an elegant wooden trunk with brass straps? For traveling to Europe?"

"Only if it can fit in our stateroom on the 747," Jaeger said.

It took Peter time to understand. He had better leave. Get good sleep. He stood up.

"I'm off." He thanked them all.

His own house was icy. The fire he had left in the chunk stove had smoldered down to nothing. He built the fire up quickly and stayed near the stove until he could bear the dash to his bed. The cold there woke him for a few moments. The nails sang up their scale, the hawk called, Jane glistened. He slept.

He returned from the city and Poughkeepsie with his rosewood and mahogany and ash and butternut and racked it up carefully in the new room, shimming each piece of wood up so air could circulate all around it. In time there would be a special shed only for the wood, where he could dry it for years and open it up and discover his ideas in the wood unhurriedly.

The warming came. He finished the sheathing of the house, the siding and the shingled roof and the casements. He completed the wiring and got the hot water working. Arranged his tools, aligned his machines. Began. The harness he had chosen to pull in was softening into his shape, his sweat annealing it, making this life pliable. And he fished early and late in the legendary Battenkill that flowed out of Vermont all across his country to empty into the Hudson. He had been a warm-water fisherman, plugging for bass in the weedy ponds and lethargic lakes of the Ohio he had grown up in; but he had learned about trout and salmon in the spuming rills of Sweden, and now he would fish no other way. The water of the Battenkill was dropping quickly without the wet spring of other years, and the warm May had spawned hatch after hatch of the Ephemerida on schedule. He had taken many large browns with predictability. Twice he had driven to Jane's house to give her fish, but she was not home.

By the end of May, for all his work on the building, he had still completed three pieces. A large box-like drawer within its own stand for holding a silver service, and two extremely narrow bookcases, eighteen inches wide by five feet high. The box for the silver was done in pearwood, the bookcases in lemonwood. Every morning he rubbed them with oils of his own device. And he had completed the pine hutch and delivered it to Jaeger.

Jaeger had offered him his choice from among twenty canvases. They were all broad, feathery abstractions in flat, pastel-light colors. Each painting seemed as if it were one piece of a large, endless roll. Twenty pieces. Nothing appealed to him. He pointed at random. "Yours," Jaeger had said. There was also the bill for seventy dollars for the wood and the stain and the varnish. Jaeger was surprised at the cost. Now the picture leaned against the wall across from his three pieces.

He heard the car coming up the road. Even over the whine of his bandsaw he heard the car exploding up the hill. He turned off the saw and watched as she stopped at his mailbox and took out his mail for him and then started up his driveway.

"Who is Heldogras?" she asked, handing him letters, catalogs, *The Wise Shopper.* She walked by him into the room and turned around and around in it admiringly, and then she saw the three pieces. "Oh," she said, and went to them. Her hand moved to touch them, but she took it back. She wanted to touch them but would not.

"Go ahead," he said from the doorway. "Go ahead."

She reached out her hand and drew it across the wide top of the box for the silver. "I've never felt wood like this," she said. "It's velvety. Softer. Is this all one piece?"

"No." He walked over to her. "It's two pieces. I joined them. You can't even see the line. The joint mostly follows the grain. You can't even feel it, the joint."

"I know," she said. She rubbed the piece again.

"Not that way," he said. "Here's the way to tell how close a joint is. With your tongue." He bent to the case and touched the tip of his tongue to where the joint should be. He stood up. "If you can't feel a joint with your tongue, then there is no joint any longer."

She bent to the case and licked it. "Peuh." She made a face. "It tastes terrible. It tastes like your coffee."

"You're not supposed to taste it, just feel it."

"Peuh," she said.

And then they stood on either side of the furniture.

"How have you been? How's your back?"

He told her how he had been and where he was now, getting his motion, moving well. Sixteen hours a day. By summer's end he was certain he could fill the shop with pieces. And he was going to do a harpsichord case, the wooden work, all in yellow Andaman padouk. He had heard from a friend in Sweden that the Andaman padouk was being sold. It was wood that had belonged to an old cabinetmaker in Sigtuna, northwest of Stockholm, as rare as wood could be. He and his friend had often tried to buy the wood, but the old man would not sell it. And now he was dead and his daughter was going to sell it and between the two of them, him and his friend, they had bought it.

"There isn't that much of it. I couldn't afford it if there was. I'll only get about 300 board feet, but even with a good ten percent wastage, fifteen even, I'll have enough for the harpsichord and a bench. And I already know the wood. I know just what I can expect from it. It's being shipped next week. This is very exciting, do you see? Getting this wood? I never thought it would happen." Could a writer understand this? "You don't know about this kind of experience," he said. "This is a different kind of reality."

"Is that your friend? Heldogras? The one who is buying the wood with you?" It was not a question. It was something else.

"Heldogras is a friend, but a different friend. A different *kind* of friend, all right?" His voice had tightened.

"I'm sorry. I pry. It's not personal. I pry. That's my kind of reality. A letter from Sweden. A woman's handwriting. I go on from there. I'm sorry. I really am."

"Like Trigorin?" he said.

"You listened to that?"

"I listened. I just didn't understand."

They were silent again. She turned to the thin bookcases. "Are these expensive?"

"Two hundred dollars."

"Where do I lick them?" But he did not answer. "Hey," she said, turning to him. "You aren't really angry, are you? Don't be angry. I've got me some good news and I'm delivering it around the countryside. I'm bursting with self-congratulations. I sold a story to *Sewanee Review*. $400." She flared up. "I'm going to eat all next year." She punched him on the arm. "Come on. Let's go to Saratoga. I'll buy you lunch. I'll show you the town. Come on."

"You're always feeding me," he said.

Then she saw Jaeger's painting. "Did you do the hutch? But of course you did. Jaeger wouldn't have given you the painting first." She walked over to the painting. "What do you think?"

"No more trades," he said.

She turned and ran over to him. "Good. No more trades. No deals. But this is different. This is a treat. A celebration. I *need* it. Come on. Come *on.*"

They drove to Saratoga, twenty miles westward, and she took him to an elegant lunch at Lillian's on Broadway. And after lunch she walked him about the town like a tour guide, showing him bookstores and the coffee house where young musicians played and poets read their work, galleries and leather shops and bitter-tasting springs. The library, the bakery, the museum in the park.

She was tall, nearly as tall as he, and a little slouchy in a loose, big-boned way. She moved quickly, the quickness of energy and not nerves, so she seemed to take up more space than other people, to live in a kind of swirling. In Lillian's, along the streets of Saratoga, in its stores, she captured wherever she was. Crossing one street she took his arm unconsciously and hugged it, a gesture out of the general exuberance that fueled her, an affection for the world coming out according to her plan, which was no plan more than to go on as she was. "Oh Peter," she said across the street. But nothing more. She dropped his arm. She smacked her fist into her palm and walked on in seven-league strides, her peasant skirt caught against her long, driving thighs, her black hair free again. He trotted to catch her.

She gave him advice. He must advertise. Seek outlets in Albany and Glens Falls. Go to the important crafts fairs like the one at Rhinebeck. And above all he would have to contact interior decorators. They were the people who really sold the hand-crafted furniture. And he would need an accountant to do his taxes. An accountant could save him a fortune. She would recommend the accountant that she used. She seemed to know all about surviving.

The day turned longer, exfoliated. She took him to antiques and to a lady who raised and sold African violets from under the fluorescent lights in her basement. There were hundreds of plants and Jane bought six of them. And one for him. "They're good plants for taking care of themselves," she said.

They drove six miles down to Ballston Spa so she could show him some special buildings, cupolas that would never be built again and upper stories that overhung the sidewalk. And back to Saratoga. They decided to stay for a six o'clock movie at the Community.

"The country mice come to town," she said. She did not want to stop. Nor did he.

The day was good for him. Other than fishing, he had been working all through the week, free from days, on the house and the furniture. And on his ideas. Only the ideas were difficult, insubstantial and without a grain to consider or a place to cut into. A few days earlier he had hiked up to the top of his land to think about his strategy and his checkbook, but the day, just then, just there, kept him on the hilltop and away from the future.

He thought about his future just enough to get by. There was money to finish off the extension and the repairs to the house. There was about five hundred dollars for incidental pieces of equipment and supplies that he might need. He had wood enough for now. And there was a few hundred more for food and gas. The money for the harpsichord had come out of that. Sooner or later he would sell something, and then something else. It would take time. He had no illusions that way. He would achieve solvency after he was ready, prepared. First things first.

But it was good for him now to be listening to Jane. He did not know his details and she did. His future took on some of her heat and exactness.

"Can you do restorations? You know, replace missing legs, heal cracks or whatever, that sort of thing? Can you make fancy picture frames?"

"Yes. I can carve wood, too, but . . ." She pushed him aside.

"Well, there you are. Get people to know that. Get people to know that you exist. Listen, I've got an idea." She pulled him into a store on Broadway that sold pottery and woven pillows and cooking gear and baskets and everything else of those kinds of things in those kinds of stores. "Ask him," she whispered sharply to him after she had told the salesgirl that they would like to see the owner and the girl had gone off to get him.

"Ask him what?" What had she done?

"You know. If they want something. *Something made of wood.*" She poked him hard in the ribs, his conspirator.

The owner appeared. Peter explained that he was a furniture maker: chairs, chests, music stands, anything else. His own designs, the best of woods. The owner of the store asked his price range.

"Look," the owner said. "I don't sell that kind of thing. People come in here, they're looking for a present. Ten dollars, twenty. Maybe even fifty. What about bowls? Can you show me some turned bowls?"

"And boxes?" Jane asked. "What about boxes? He makes terrific boxes."

"Yeah, I'll look at some boxes, too."

"Would you consider taking a bookcase on consignment? Two hundred dollars?" she asked him. She nodded at him to encourage him.

"On consignment? Why not?" the owner said.

Peter said, "Wait a minute," but Jane dragged him out of the store. Outside. "What are you doing? I don't want to turn bowls. I don't want to make a lot of boxes. And I don't want to put the bookcase in a knickknack store."

"Why not? As long as you make it well, what do you care who buys it or how it's sold? This way people will at least get to see your work. They'll see the bookcase in the window and ask who made it. What's wrong with that? What's wrong with *you*?"

"Would you write bowls?"

"No," she said quickly.

"So?"

"So *what*? I don't follow you."

"You don't follow *me*? *I* don't follow *you*!"

"It's different," she said.

"Why, because you sold a story today? Because you're going to eat all year?"

"It's different," she repeated.

"How?"

"You don't care," she said. "It's all the same to you. You make something and you sell it and it's gone."

"That's outrageous."

"It's not an insult, Peter, just a fact."

"It is *not* a fact, and it's still outrageous."

"Well, what do you want, then?" she said. "And anyway, you don't have to do any of this. All you did was find out something, that's all."

And it was good for him to find out something. He had always known that he would need to know more than wood and his skills to live from them, but he did not know what more. Out on his mountain he would never find out. He needed the ballast of this marketplace, some lead in his life, a chance to come down from Sweden and the harpsichord into the valley. A chance to come down from his hilltop, up where he could not care.

After the movie they had a beer in a downstairs bar on Caroline Street in the center of town.

"I'll make some boxes but I won't turn bowls," he said across the table to her. She leaned back hard against the booth seat, shaking it. Laughing, she reached out and put both her hands on top of his, nearly spilling the beer between them, and squeezed firmly.

"Is that what you were thinking during the movie?"

"It was a lousy movie."

She had put on her glasses in the movie and wore them still. Looking at her, he could see himself reflected in the lenses, and that small reflection stuck within the background of what seemed her gigantic eyes, his head and shoulders and chest fixed within her dilated pupils. Her hands were rougher than ever from the gardening, and her face, still smooth as ceramic, was darkening from the sun.

They drove home. In two days she was going to Shreveport, Louisiana, to be part of a creative writing workshop sponsored by the state university. Ten days. The minor leagues. Her fee would cover travel expenses and she might clear a few hundred beyond that. It was thankless work but part of her life, the steps before the giant steps. Shreveport before Bread Loaf. My bowls, she told him. Not even boxes.

They drove back through the soft night off the uplifted limestone strata of Saratoga down onto the sandy plain by the Hudson and then across the river and up the rising, enfolded shale hills eastward. They talked on about what they were doing, would do now. Their tempos suddenly leaped in a coda to their day, quick recapitulation, intense upward modulation. Ideas of shape, of ordering so clearly etched occurred to them each that their hearts raced separately toward the morning, when they could work.

At the bottom of his hill she slowed in order to make the acute-angled turn up his road, but he told her he would walk it, take the night air. She stopped the car; the engine running down chattered the loose body. In the silence the peepers still chirped, but bullfrogs called now, too, up from the light streams feeding the Battenkill. He did not get out. She waited. But their metaphors came between them, just then, and bound them like the indenturing vows of apprentices to tasks and to other glories.

"Thank you," he said outside the car. "A great day." He turned and crunched off into the darkness. The car exploded and shuddered away.

He followed as much of her advice as he could. He would wait to advertise when he had more pieces to show, but he checked out interior decorators in the Albany area in the telephone directory from the Greenwich library. He called some of them and sent letters to others telling them what he had to offer. He turned three bowls out of some blocks of cherry that he had, and he constructed three clean and simple boxes, three by four by seven inches, out of scraps of various things. He took them to the store on Broadway and sold them immediately, eight dollars for each bowl, six dollars for each box: forty-two dollars. The owner said to bring him more, and asked about the bookcase. Peter said he would bring it in next time.

Forty-two dollars and a painting. His gross profit. Something had begun, but what? He would drive by Jane's again. Often now when he was out he would drive by her house on Christie Road to check on it. He supposed that Mara fed the cat. He would stop his truck at her house and try both doors and walk about. Three days after he had expected her to return and she had not, he began to drive by the house each day. At the end of a week he stopped at the Jaegers' to ask if they had heard from her. Could something be wrong? Should something be done?

"Jane can take care of herself," Mara said. "She probably stopped somewhere to visit friends. She often does." Then she said, "Are you interested in her?"

"Interested?"

"Oh, you know what I mean."

But he had left that alone and driven off.

And now, two weeks past due, she was back. He pulled into

the driveway to tell her how he had earned some money at last. She was in the garden, hoeing furiously, desperately, he thought. She swung the hoe like a pick. The dirt splattered. He meant to say hello. Instead he said, "What's wrong?"

She looked up at him from under her wide-brimmed straw fieldhand's hat. It set off her face nicely, pulling her features into a frame, holding them together as they were not naturally held together.

"Well, the garden for one thing," she said. She was tired. She was trying to drive her tiredness into the ground. She would stay in the hot garden all day until it was dark, and then she would be exhausted and would sleep and would wake up tomorrow and start again, and maybe after she did that for enough days she would be able to be still again, in balance.

"And for another thing?" he asked. He had wanted this to be a greeting for both of them, a returning.

But she was not through with the garden. "Look at the lettuce. Didn't it rain here at *all*?" She dropped to her knees and straddled the row, her fingers scurrying like mice through the wilted stems, plucking out the hopeless.

"It's not my fault. I can't control that."

She looked up at him. "What are you talking about?"

"The rain. I couldn't make it rain. I'm sorry, it's one of my weaknesses." He was shouting.

"Stop shouting. Don't you shout at me." She shook her fist at him. She stood up and took her hoe over to the cauliflower, away from him. The pastel-green leaves were erect and firm. They had set well. She worked between the widely spaced plants, scraping the low-sprouting purslane off the dirt like icing off a cake. He followed her.

"I only stopped by to tell you I sold some bowls and boxes. To that store in Saratoga. He wants more." He waited close behind her. She did not turn.

"That's fine," she said in her smallest voice. By her left foot he saw a bead of water drop in the dust on a waxy cauliflower leaf. A tear.

"Go away, Peter. Leave me alone for a while, OK?"

Instead he put an arm around her and walked her out of the garden to her back porch and sat down with her. He put his other hand up to her face. Her hat fell off. He eased her head down to him and let her sob into him. The cat purred by, rubbing against her. Back and forth the cat went, purring louder and louder until they could both feel the cat vibrating against them.

"How much did you get for the bowls and boxes?" she asked.

"Forty-two dollars."

"That's not bad, is it?" She sat up from him. She began to figure. "You could almost live a week on that, couldn't you?" She pushed her hair back.

"Maybe. If I had a garden," he smiled.

She took his hand. "I've got more than enough. I grow enough for a dozen people. You can't just grow one tomato plant. Get a freezer. I'll show you what to do."

"Sure," he said. "OK. And next time I'll water the lettuce." She squeezed his hand and let it drop. She picked up her hat and put it on.

"This hat does wonders for me. I don't look half bad in this hat, you know." She went back into the garden and he went with her. She got him another hoe and showed him what to do.

Shreveport had been terrible. What she had expected, but worse, too. The heat, the impossible food, the ship of fools she had been sent to sea in. What most depleted her was the pretentiousness and vulgarity of it all. She had not expected talent or skill; only a reasonable willingness to talk intelligently about fiction, about how people thought and felt their way through the human predicament. She had not been even remotely close. They had come to strut and to pretend. A retired doctor who was going to cash in on forty years of his patients' confidences. Cash in. That about summed them up. On the fifth day the doctor had propositioned her, had actually offered her money.

"No kidding? Wow. What did he offer? What are you worth on the open market?"

"That's not the end of it. Michael Lerner, the poet who was doing the poetry part of the workshop, he wanted me for *nothing.* He was going to do me a favor, the vain asshole."

"He was going to charge you, huh?"

She hacked at the weeds and the dirt.

"Maybe you're angry because he valued you too low. The doctor didn't offer enough, the poet didn't offer anything. Your feelings are hurt."

She refused his joke. "Then there were two creeps taking the fiction workshop who were always hanging around me, too. Fifty-year-old men in tight blue jeans. They had to alter the jeans to get their guts in. And it was like they just read Kerouac, for godssake. Long hair, sunglasses, grass, fat men in blue jeans drinking beer and talking *street* in Shreveport, Louisiana, in the good old summertime. Damn. Every time I turned around, there they were."

"I don't know. It sounds kind of flattering, all that attention."

"Does it?" she said, sharply enough so that he looked up. She had crossed over into his row and now confronted him. "Does it? The only bitch in town?"

"Hey, come on, will you. I'm making a joke. I'm trying to cheer you up." And he tried again. "You know how it is with you arty types."

"You're such an innocent?" The air between them cracked open. He did not like the smell of this talk about the men around her, and she knew it. In the broken air between them he saw her looking at him just as he was looking at her, the sunlight silvering them both like mirrors. "What about Sweden? What about Heldogras?" she said.

"What?" It was shocking.

But she turned away and went back to cultivating her row. She was past the cauliflower now and into the broccoli, moving fast.

He recovered. That she had remembered Heldogras had surprised him. Confused him. She imagined things so differently than he. "Heldogras was something else altogether. You can't compare . . ." But she was not listening. She would not hear. Even in the briskly rising heat of this day, she was huddled coldly in her trouble, larger than Shreveport.

They worked without talking, with only the sound of their hoes slurring through the dirt connecting them. He tried to match his stroke to hers, catching her rhythm, so they were raising and dropping their hoes exactly together. She finished her row and waited for him.

"I stopped in Washington," she said when she was next to him. His blue shirt was dark with sweat. "I visited good friends. College friends. Bill and Helen Wells. We were all together in Bennington. They got married right after college. The week after. Now they're talking separation. Divorce. It was ghastly. They're living together and they're thinking about divorce. They still sleep in the same bed, use the same john, and any day they might split. I didn't know how to handle it. I was in agony. There I was on the living room couch, like whenever I visited. Only it was like none of us belonged there any longer. We had gotten stuck together in the past and couldn't get loose in the present."

"Why didn't you just leave?"

"They wouldn't let me. I had to listen to one, then the other. Alone. And then together. Over and over. Like it was their hobby. And maybe I was fascinated, too. I'm not allowed to turn away from anything. Anyway, it was all quiet and urbane. Civilized. It was so civilized now that I couldn't understand how they could have married in the first place. Where was passion? Where was the anger in their disappointment? Peter, shouldn't they have been hurt or angry?"

"There aren't any rules," he said.

"I think there are," she said. "They just didn't play by them."

"It comes out to the same thing," he said. But she shook her head against that, dull and heavy.

"Do you want some iced tea? I do. I've got it ready."

They sat on the edge of the back porch and drank the tea, thick and minty. He had taken off his shirt to the sun.

She said, "Do you know what I saw this morning? I saw a Canada goose. Just one. It was flying south. Incredible. That really upset me."

"How do you know it was a goose? They fly so high, you can hardly tell it's a goose from just one bird. You need a flock in a V to tell."

"Oh sure you can tell. You can see the wing beat. Nothing flies like a Canada goose. I could tell."

"Maybe it was just flying around. South for just a little, but then it was going to turn back north and catch up with the flock. You can't tell."

"I could tell. It was going south. All alone. It was very upsetting."

"You *couldn't* tell," he insisted. "Anyway, animals are always doing strange things." He turned his head to her. "Breaking rules." She was staring out across the garden to the long arbor of grapes that marked the north boundary of her property. "And why should something like that upset you?"

She put her hand, her fingers, on the scar on his back. It was white and twisted like a mealworm, and the skin beside it was pink and tender. She rubbed it absently.

"Oh Peter, I can't get an agent to handle my novel. A third agent turned it down." She rubbed the scar softly, as if she would make it go away. Her hand was not as calloused or tight as it had been before she had gone to Shreveport.

"Can't you just send it to a publisher yourself?"

"Yes, but novels never get bought that way. I need an agent and I can't even get one."

"You've only tried three."

"Three's enough. That tells you something."

"That's silly. You can't just give up."

"I know. I can't give up but right now I feel like I can't win. Like my friends in Washington. My life's like a Mexican standoff." She was rubbing his whole back now with two hands, massaging it, but she did not know how. He had learned how in Sweden.

"You're tired, that's all. You're just down. A little depressed. You need some rest and then you'll go on. You know that. Rejections are part of the game. Your whole life is going to be like this. It won't stop, you know." Her hands stopped. He turned completely around to face her and put down his glass of iced tea. She looked at him dumbly, her mouth half opened to say something, as if she had been struck across the face. Her eyes were wet again, and her dark hair framed her face within the frame of the hat.

"Hey, Janie," he said quietly. "It's just not so bad. You'll be OK. You'll see." He put his hands around her neck and slowly worked his fingers into her muscles as Heldogras had taught him. Finding the knots, he kneaded her and she loosened. Then her tears came slowly.

"Goddamn bird," she said.

He unbuttoned her shirt and opened it and bent to her chest and kissed each small breast. She closed him in her arms and rocked back with him onto the porch. He kissed her all over her face, gently, over and over. Then, "Peter," she said. "Don't do this now." She was hugging him tightly. He tried to push up from her but she had not released him. "Peter?" She was asking something. "Are you going to be angry?"

"No," he said. "I'm just going to be mixed up." She opened her arms.

Standing by his truck she said, "It's not you. I like you. It's just that I can't rest now. Yet." He started the truck. "I'm not making this clear, am I?"

"No. You're not. Do you think *you've* got it clear? What do you mean 'rest'?"

"Peter, it's just that I suddenly saw my life, just then, about to turn into something I might write."

"Trigorin again?"

"No. Not Trigorin. You. You said it yourself. You didn't want to find yourself in a story. That's what I felt back there."

"Janie, I really don't understand this. I'm not angry. I'm not hurt. I like you, too. I just don't understand what the hell is going on." He started to back out. She had to step away.

"You'll come back here, won't you? You won't stay away because of this, will you?"

"Sure. I'll come back whenever you want." He backed out onto Christie Road and drove off to his own work.

But after a week he had not heard from her and he went back. She was gone again. He walked around the house and checked the doors. The garden was getting weedy again. Before she had left she had mulched the tomatoes and heavier plants, but the seedlings were shaggy. He unwound the hose from its reel against the side of the house and watered the lettuce soakingly and wetted down the rest of the garden as well. He finished watering as Mara drove up. From the road she called.

"Here. I was heading your way." She waved an envelope at him through her car window. "And Jaeger wants to talk to you. He's up at the house now. See you later." She drove off.

The note was from Jane. She had enclosed it in a letter to Mara to save time.

> Peter, I am on Long Island doing work, would you believe it? Got called away urgently. Great possibility. Will explain when I see you. Do me a favor? Save my garden? Water the lettuce like you promised. And remember, half of everything you save is yours. The Law of Salvage, I think. The key to the house is on the ledge above the back door. I like you a whole lot.
>
> Jane

He went back into the garden and weeded in it for an hour. He picked some radishes and lettuce for lunch. Then he went further up the road to Jaeger.

Jaeger wanted to add a small room to his house, a breakfast nook off the kitchen. He wanted Peter to do it.

"You can do it, can't you? This sort of thing?"

"Yes, I can do it, but not for paintings."

"Oh no no no, of course not. Draw me some pictures and give me an estimate. When can you do it? I'd like to get this done as soon as possible."

"Now. I can do it now."

"You can?"

"Sure. Get me a ruler and some paper."

In an hour he had sketched out the addition and shown Jaeger what his options were: windows here or there, baseboard electric heating or not, lighting possibilities, built-in seats. He figured he could do it for about three thousand dollars, half material, half labor. Jaeger said go ahead.

"Shake," Jaeger said. Then Peter thought that Jaeger must also have had the job estimated by someone else. He had underbid.

"You'll have to pay for the materials first," Peter said. "I don't have the money to lay out. You can put a check in the safe at Curtiss Building Supplies and I'll draw materials against it. OK?"

"Fine. I'll do that today. When can you start?"

"Tomorrow."

But tomorrow it rained. It rained for two days. The lettuce would survive without him. He stayed in his workshop and turned bowls and worked on some boxes. A hundred dollars' worth. On the third day he started the addition to Jaeger's house. He contracted for a back-hoe to dig the foundation trench, and by the afternoon he had set the forms for the concrete footing and had called in the Redi-mix truck. By the end of the day he had finished the footing and was ready to lay up the concrete blocks of the foundation. In three days he would have the deck down and completed; the rest of the building would be easier, closer to making furniture where you could work on a piece at a time, measure and cut and fit precisely. The rest of the addition he could work in around his own work. And his garden. Driving home that night he stopped at Jane's house, but only for a moment. Then he returned to his hill.

On the second night he stayed at Jane's. It saved him the drive home and back to Jaeger's in the morning. He sat on the back porch and drank a beer and watched a large woodchuck circle up to the fenced-in squash, the courgette. It sniffed the fence and then waddled back into the field. He thought he should get a .22 and sit here and drink beer at the end of a good working day and plink woodchucks. The thought rode over him pleasantly like sleep when it is good. He finished his beer and then worked in the garden until the mosquitoes began to come up too quickly. Then he went into the house and showered and made himself a tuna salad.

When he had come to his hill the first thing he had had to learn was what to do with his nights. At first he had been too tired out from his work and excitement: his days and nights did not break up into busy-ness and loneliness, only into light and dark. But soon enough he found his day ending and then nothing else. He had expected that. It was part of the overall equation—the money, the land, the tools, the wood, the loneliness. And the time to work on it all, that was part of the equation, too. It would take time to blend everything into a life, to make the accommodations that would be needed, and to add what he would find as he went along.

He got a TV. He hooked together his tape deck and equipment and speakers. He read more. And he worked at his drawing board on his designs. Some nights he would go over to a roadhouse in Salem and listen to good hillbilly music and to the people, farmhands and millworkers mostly, getting slowly and happily drunk. But most of all he waited.

His first night at Jane's he examined Frederick Whinney's house closely, happier even than the first time to discover unexpected intricacies and details. Had Whinney done this because of his grandmother, or to spite her? After the eleven o'clock news, he got into Jane's bed and slept.

Days followed days. It rained more than he had counted on. He turned bowls and sold them. Closed in Jaeger's addition. Took off a bright day following the rain to bring the garden up to prime. Blossoming was everywhere. Fruits were forming—beans, early tomatoes, broccoli, cauliflower. Jane sent a letter instructing him to harvest the peas, how to blanch and freeze them, which were the snow peas to be treated specially. How to tie the cauliflower leaves up around their heads. To hill the potatoes and the onions and the leeks. And more.

> I'm into the planning of a huge writing project. Who knows when I'll return, but very soon, I hope. Oh, I miss my garden. Do take care of it, and I hope it isn't taking up your life. In haste.
>
> Jane

Three weeks. He sat on the back porch drinking beer. The woodchuck came up to the fence in its ritual of hope. It had dug down, but Jane had set the fence deep. And after that the woodchuck had no other strategies, only patience and hope that one day the fence would be gone.

He drank his beer. The addition was finished. A friend of Jaeger's wanted him to turn his one-car garage into a two-car garage. Another friend wanted him to fix a leak in the roof. The store in Saratoga wanted as many bowls and boxes as he could reasonably produce. They were selling well. August was coming. The racing season. The tourists.

He sat on the back porch in the sun's long rays, drinking the beer. Already the summer had started to break up into a hazy layering, the diminishing curve of spring's excited becoming flattening down into methodical and even growth. A tree in the hills across the river had burst into accidental autumn fire, while the dark and vital green of all the trees grayed down beneath the wax thickening over their leaves to protect against the dog-day heat to come.

He heard the car. At first he thought it was a memory, a trick of memory in a daydream, but it was real enough and approached. Even before it arrived, he went around to the front of the house and waited.

She threw her arms all over him. She hugged him and then came back to hug him again.

"You look great," he said. She was deeply tanned. Even her dark hair had tinted auburn. "You really do. You look like a piece of well-rubbed beech." He reached and rubbed her cheek across the bone. "Come and see your garden." He took her hand and they ran to the rear of the house into the field. He showed her through it, explaining what he had done with her instructions and what he had contrived on his own.

"Oh you've done well," she said. "I couldn't have done better." She examined everything, the distance he had thinned the carrots, how he had trained up the cucumber vines, if the melons were finding themselves enough sun. She pinched the soil to see if it was friable and yet damp. "Should I be happy or jealous? You've done so well with it."

"You could be both, I guess."

She took his arm and pranced him into her house. He was everywhere in it. His clothing, his books and papers, his slight rearrangement of pots and dishes and knives in the kitchen. His impress was upon it all. A chair shifted, the cat's dish placed to the left of the door, the TV moved a foot nearer to the sofa. His smell. So quickly he had possessed her house, assumed her garden.

"What are you doing?" she asked. He was hunkered down before the open refrigerator, considering it. How broad he was across the back! She had forgotten that, or perhaps never remarked it. How tight limbed!

"Making you something to eat," he said. "I'll bet you didn't eat all day. I hardly ate all day myself." But then he stood up from the refrigerator and closed it. He came to the table and sat down across from her. "I'm just so glad you're back," he said. Then he sat and watched her, smiling and still.

"Me too," she said. "Me too."

But she was not *back*. For the weeks that she had been gone, she had not wanted to be gone, had wanted badly to be here, to come back. She had counted on it through the tiring collisions of the work sessions on the project, and even more through the shrill excursions of the talented and skilled people unfurled in their flags and ensigns of social array, drinking and talking hard, as strained as if they were always sailing close reached, stiffly, in an endless race. But what she had come back to now seemed gone, moved forward to where she had just caught up with it, a goodness, yes, but of another kind. *What kind?* She fluttered at the answer.

"I'll do it," she said, getting up. "It's been so long. I miss my kitchen."

"I'll help. I'll get things from the garden. You get settled."

From the kitchen window she watched him move about with the woven ash-split basket, picking delicately through and across the long rows. She put her knuckle between her teeth. She had imagined this, exactly this scene, at night in Amagansett after the restless and nervous house of her hostess had subsided and still she could not sleep. She would look out her kitchen window at her rich garden and then he would be in it, working in it as she had told him in her letters, moving about in an inland light so different from that of the sea. Even today, driving the long trip home, she had imagined this again. She trembled, actually grasped the edge of the table to still herself.

She had made something come true.

They worked together. He had gathered cucumbers, early tomatoes, baby carrots, a small cauliflower, young broccoli, Swiss chard, lettuce that he had shaded from the sun, tender yellow wax beans, scallions, a cutting of chives. He stripped cold chicken from bones in the refrigerator and made the salad and a hot and garlicy French dressing while she steamed the beans and stir-fried almost everything else in olive oil. They heated frozen rolls in the toaster oven.

"This is good, this is so good," she said. "They eat so badly out there. Good, but bad, you know what I mean? Everyone's worried about their health but they eat steaks like this," she showed him how thick, "and pounds of lobster in pounds of butter. And the drinking. Wow." She ate quickly. "This salad dressing is terrific. Oops." She dribbled some food out the side of her mouth. He got up and snapped a paper towel from its roll for her. She saw him watching her. He ate slowly. He is ruminating, she thought. What a word.

She was repossessing nothing. He had jumped her claim.

She told him what had gotten her to Amagansett. A college friend had landed a contract with Hawthorn to do a book on American regions. The subject wasn't new, but the approach would be. The approach had sold it. The idea was to build a grid of universal activities and then to lay it on the seasons and the place. "For instance, road-building and maintenance through the seasons in all the regions of the country. Do you get it? You can't see America unless you see its people at work against the backdrop of their two most important influences, terrain and weather. How about that?"

"It sounds like a good idea. Where do you fit in?"

"I'm going to do this part of the country. Upstate New York and thereabouts. I'll have to travel sometimes, but mostly I'll be here."

"I thought you wrote fiction."

"I *write,*" she said. "Mostly I write fiction, but sometimes other things. It's not either/or. And if this works out I'll make some real money, which I can use. It's a good experience."

"You don't have to defend it. Not to me. You're defending it and you don't have to."

"Yes I do," she said. "A little. Sometimes a lot."

"No you don't. You're too up or down. You should level off."

"There goes my Nobel Prize."

"See. See. All or nothing with you."

"I was just kidding, Peter. I thought all about this project before I accepted. I'll *like* doing it, honest. I'm OK. I'm all right."

He told her about building the addition for Jaeger and the work he was going to do on Jaeger's friend's garage. He was also producing an easy one hundred dollars' worth of bowls a week for the Saratoga store. He would work on his fine pieces in the winter, when the tourists were gone and the weather closed off his construction work. He would build the harpsichord then.

They had chocolate ice cream for dessert. She told him stories about the high life far out on Long Island. He brought her up to date on Washington County. "In some ways it's not all that different," she said.

"In the meantime, I'm rolling in money." He showed her his accounts scribbled on a piece of paper in his wallet.

"You shouldn't do it that way. Here." She showed him her carefully kept account ledger and the envelopes of specific receipts. "You'll need these for the accountant. Did you call the accountant yet?" He hadn't, but would. He was thinking of buying a mortar mixer. What kind of write-off could he get? The accountant would know.

He had left the mat in the tub after showering and it had gotten moldy underneath. He had mixed meat and fish scraps in with the vegetable trimmings for the compost heap. She found an empty beer can under the sofa in the living room, and small plaques of dried mud in the hallway, even though he had swept from time to time. He was all around her, like a fume.

At ten o'clock he said he would go. He went to gather his clothes. But even if he took everything of his away, he would continue in the house now, like a stain.

"Peter," she called after him through the short L-shaped hall. "Stay."

She woke early. The redwings and grackles were signaling to each other from the verges of nearly dried-up streams. Sparrows, wrens, thrushes bubbled about. It would be a hot day. Already the heat had stirred enough insects into flight that the barn swallows sailed about, plucking them out of the air. The birds were in place. She awoke and stretched out and bumped him. He stirred but slept on, deep, completed, creasing the bed downward. In the room's dim light his white scar glowed. She rolled toward him and kissed the scar and fell back. She smiled at the ceiling. There was so much to do. The garden would need harvesting in earnest this year. And she did not want to lose the summer interviews for the book. She had thought of enough likely possibilities already to get her going, and once she started she could keep on. She would find the others. There was so much to do. She should get up and begin. Still, she waited in the day rising, waited for them, by degrees, to dwindle into lovers. And maybe less.

The Rags of Time

> Awake, O north wind; and come, thou South;
> blow upon my garden, that the spice thereof
> may flow out. Let my beloved come into
> his garden, and eat his pleasant fruits.

Twice a week Thomas Wilkens's passion raged up in him, pounding and beating against his ribs like a violent bird that, even after weeks of captivity, could not comprehend or abide its cage.

At 1:30 on Tuesday and Thursday afternoons Fay Lester would slam her way, always nearly late, into his class in seventeenth-century English poetry, her hips moving in a flippant bounce of scorn for the way flesh goes.

Why me? Wilkens had wondered to himself when the first hot blast of infatuation had blown across the decorous, well-tended garden of his life and withered it. He had held up to the mid-afternoon sun the hands with which he had tended that garden, had brought them close to his eyes so that he could see the blood-red light through the edges of his fingers. His hands, like his career, like his life, were thin and translucent, soft but precise, well defined. Until now. He had clapped his fingers to his eyes against what he saw, but nothing could darken the self-illuminating madness he tumbled into now. Or was it love?

Love? What had he to do with love? A man of calm and propriety, he had fallen to a slow but enormous poison, that was all; so who was he, Thomas Wilkens, to ask, "Why me?" Who, he asked, are any of us to ask such questions of flesh, especially when the flesh brazenly announced itself to be Fay Lester?

Wilkens sat in his gracious carpeted office in the new faculty building and looked out across the neat, groomed campus sloping down to the bordering village of Cobbton. Between the village and the campus, in the thick buffering band of maples, was his house, near and far enough for him to bike between when the weather was right, a sedate rider erect on his old three-speed Raleigh, his muffler streaming out behind him in the downhill wind, a nearly anachronistic picture of the professor that he had preserved from an old English film he had once seen, a slight affectation, the smallest permission of whimsy.

In November, when all the leaves were gone, he could make out which home was his, for in Cobbton the houses were elegantly old and individually conceived and far apart. He could see the high, turreted room in which Neil, his elder son, sixteen, crashed about in his life just now, arrogant and befuddled by fits and starts as his body thickened and his thoughts turned.

He and Mildred had wanted the large round-turreted room for themselves. A hundred years before, the room had been designed for the masters; when they had purchased the house ten years ago, the year after he had gotten tenure and been promoted to associate professor, it was that room with all its windows and difficulties (where did anything go in a round room?) that had convinced them. The boys slept together then on the second floor.

But at fourteen Neil had won the room from them, his need for a private territory driving them out. On the other hand, it was their way of containing, of isolating, him. Let his musics and his banners and his fantasies be in one place. Let there be a precise boundary between Neil's maddening life and their own so that there could continue to *be* a life of their own. For the tale was too old for telling.

In his own high school days there had been a cheerleader taller, blonder, prettier than the rest, who answered to the crowds she exhorted as though she was the one they cheered for, rather than the Egremont High School football team out there on the muddy field behind her. And she was right. Nor was this a vain and conscious egotism; she was as lovely and alive, destined for adulation as swirling hawks and yellowing oaks and summer sunsets are destined. She was the epitome of what all the lesser girls prancing beside her were supposed to be, what women everywhere were aiming at. And the crowds that lived vicariously in the warriors clashing on the field lived vicariously in her as well.

She alone wore earrings to the game, droplets of gold dangling on delicate chains, and when she swung her head to the rhythm of the chanting ritual cadences, the eye was attracted as if to bait to the flickering gold, and to her.

For six months the young sophomore Wilkens prowled the halls of Egremont High School for daily glimpses of her. He never spoke to her. She was a senior and possessed by others. In all his masturbatory fantasies she fumed about like ether, making him drunk, knocking him out.

On the day when he had given in to Neil he had thought about that girl. Had there been others? He could not remember others, only her. By Mildred he had not been possessed. Mildred he had come to love naturally, as a man ready for life looks up one day at a pretty graduate student in the carrel across from him in the library and decides, *is* decided. He had always loved Mildred tenderly and intelligently, but never fiercely.

On the day when he had given the room to Neil he had wanted to say something that would open them to each other, but what could he say? The urgency of youth is too outrageous to be considered carefully like a poem; even to recognize it is an embarrassment. And what could there have been to say? That time and chance happeneth to all men? What would that have meant to Neil? *Did* it mean anything? But if there was nothing that he could have said to his son then, there was surely less that he could say now—not that Neil was asking or talking. Not that he was.

Wilkens looked out his office window at the pretty picture of his life. It looked just as he had hoped it would when, twenty years ago, he awoke to his last conclusion: that he was lucky and pleased to be lucky and to know, at twenty-four, what he wanted the rest of his life to be like, to know already the sweetness of contentment, leaping over the riotous excursions of youthful ambition directly into lucidity and peace. If his vision was small, at least it was well lighted.

He could remember the day, at least the sensation, when, one week after he had marched in the commencement for his master's degree at Syracuse University, old Martinson, the department chairman, had called and asked him if he could come to his home that afternoon at five o'clock. At their meeting Martinson gave him a drink and offered him a summer-school teaching job that had suddenly developed: one freshman composition course, and one survey of British literature.

He had accepted at once, although he had made elaborate plans for a free summer, his first ever, before returning to graduate school, this time to Brown and to the truly solemn ceremony of the doctoral program. But Europe could be postponed. He accepted the summer job at once because he was overwhelmed by his desire and his long, clear view of himself: to go to the library and prepare for classes, to find and organize his thoughts and words for the six weeks to come, and then for the years after, was exactly, perfectly, what he wanted to do. What Martinson offered him that afternoon was his future now—to build fine edifices and then to explain them, to organize and educate, to try to see through the prismatic imaginations of others who had taken the chances. He was glad he was himself not a writer, had never had any disposition to become one.

Teaching, of course, was what he had always expected to do, at least from his sophomore year in college. But it was more than just teaching—a calling or a career—that he had leaped to in Martinson's living room; it was a *condition,* the graceful and lucid design of a professor's life as he conceived it. That afternoon, his master's finished and nothing pending, a magma from deeper than he knew within himself had had the chance to rise to his surface, for Martinson to imprint with his massy seal. And then to cool and solidify.

That was the way it had been from then until now, a sweetly reasonable succession of life's events arranged in a languid upward curve of pleasant small accomplishments. If there was any major prospect for Wilkens to consider, other than promotion to a full professorship (and even that would come, as had everything else, in time), it was the maintenance of the way things were now, and had been; of staying what he was, becoming more of that—a stable man, clear headed, a *student* of mysteries, not a participant. He understood that about himself, the dry refinement of his mind, the limited extensions he would permit it; and that was OK, fine. He was just how he wanted to be, not smugly so, but contentedly. And there was nothing wrong with that. He made no apologies for the adequacy of his existence. Wrong, if it came to that, was the failure to live your life in terms which you could handle. Or afford. Wrong was what was going on now.

Fay Lester was neither ignorant nor rough, though after her she left that feeling in the air she had disturbed just as she left a vital scent, though she wore none.

The conference about her midterm exam had gone on for fifteen increasingly uneasy minutes, though not for her.

"But I just don't know quite what to make of this," he said. "On the first question you write well enough. You seem to understand the impact of the history of the time, of the culture, upon the poetry. You seem to understand that the literature is about the . . . the human condition as it exists at a particular moment."

He tried not to look directly at her. He would lose his way if he did that, would change the subject, become friendly, ask her about herself, about college in general, about where she came from, about books she might be reading. Drown.

"Dr. Wilkens," she said.

"What?"

"You were saying?"

But he *had* wandered. Halfway between question one and question two he had fatigued, been turned from his proper path off toward what brightly beckoned but what he could not name. Dare name. Though it had drawn him.

"The second question," he came back. "How could you manage the insights of the first question about Donne and Herbert and miss them so completely in the second?"

"It's Vaughan," she said. "Crashaw. Traherne. It's them," she explained. Then stopped as though she had, as though he understood.

"Yes," he urged, "Go on."

"I don't like them."

"But you don't have to like them. Just to understand them. That's what the exam is about—a test to see what you know to help direct you to what you should . . ."

"It's all that religion," Fay Lester said as though he had been saying nothing. "To tell you the truth it's hard for me to take, grown men believing in God and religion and all that the way they do. It just turns me off." And then, before he could answer, she added: "It just seems silly."

"Silly?"

She nodded.

He was thrilled and appalled. Whatever else they had been called, praised or blamed for, he had never heard poets of such canonical stature as Henry Vaughan or Richard Crashaw or Thomas Traherne called *silly.* He could not have imagined it happening. But there it was, Fay Lester's judgment, and what was he to do with it? Teach her? Change her mind? Defend Traherne? *Do his job for civilization and the English language?*

"Dr. Wilkens?" He had wandered off again.

"Yes. Yes. Your comment, it . . ." He raised his eyebrows and turned his mouth down and lifted his hands, palms up, to imply . . . what? Where were his words today? His weapons? "But what about Donne and Herbert? You like them. You like them a lot." He tapped her bluebook on the desk between them. "And they were religious, Lord knows. Donne was dean of St. Paul's. Herbert was a priest in the Church of England. You know that."

"Yes," Fay Lester said, not inching back at all, "but Donne and Herbert, they were better poets."

In that splendid non sequitur all, not Reason least, stood indicted.

"But Donne?" he lifted his lance against her again, but weakly. "He was a cleric. His sermons are immortal testaments to his religious belief. He was always a believer in God."

"Not in the beginning he wasn't," she came right back, instinctively prepared, alert to the nuances of a terrain that she knew well. "For God's sake hold your tongue, and let me love," Fay Lester shouted at him. She filled his office with the victory she assumed.

> Come live with me, and be my love,
> And we will some new pleasures prove
> Of golden sands, and crystal brooks:
> With silken lines, and silver hooks.

"That's no priest," she explained to him.

> Love, all alike, no season knows, nor clime,
> Nor hours, days, months, which are the rags of time.

"That's no metaphor for the *spirit* he's talking about, sir. He's talking about the *real thing.*"

The real thing. He staggered under the weight of her instruction. He glanced at his watch to avoid her. He could bear no more. There were spasms in him already that he feared.

"It's late," he said. "It's four o'clock." He leaned forward slowly and then stood up, and was surprised to find that his legs were shaky. And not surprised. But Fay Lester stayed seated. He sat down.

"To tell the truth, Dr. Wilkens, I never did think too much of priesthood and nunship. It's not natural. So the poetry that comes out isn't natural either."

"There's a body of criticism that agrees with you. In some respects. But it's not a strong argument."

"I'm not surprised," she said overriding him again. She rose at last. "See you Thursday, Dr. Wilkens." And then Fay Lester left, but was not gone.

Wilkens stayed in his chair and turned in it to look out his window at the night coming on. He struggled to float down, to release himself, to be still.

He had managed by easy stratagems to see her out of class at least once a week, casual encounters in the library or the bookstore, the college coffee hours, English Club meetings, passings between classrooms and laboratories and dorms. Three weeks ago he had begun to calculate more exactly: he had obtained from the registrar her class schedule, and, wherever it was possible for him to do so, he arranged to be somewhere near enough to see her or hear her voice or say hello or even stop and talk a moment. This afternoon he had been with her more privately for longer than ever before. He had intended their meeting to last longer yet, but he could not stand it—the possibilities bred of his imagination, the impossibilities asserted by his life.

Fay Lester had first appeared, though not as the blinding mote in his eye that she was to become, the year before, and by hearsay. He had been told at some party or other about this prince's daughter for whom Dimitri Varnov, the young Russian instructor, had cut his academic throat as far as staid Cobbton College was concerned. He, Varnov, had fallen too demonstratively in love with her, clearly enough so that his ardor became a factor to be considered in the college community's life, a factor which it did not want to consider.

Varnov was not rehired, although what had happened to him had happened to most of them once, or from time to time. To fall into infatuation with a student was to look up one ordinary day from his lecture notes, at a girl whom he suddenly looks anxiously forward to seeing again when the class meets next.

She becomes the irritating seed around which he constructs the pearl of his first vague and then specific erotic musings and dreams, the protagonistic foil to himself in his symbolic scenarios: the two of them careening off together across some empty white beach by some blue sea, free of everything. The banality of the dream itself is enticing. At last he imagines her when making love to his wife. Until one day, when she is standing next to his lectern after a class, he notices some pimples on her forehead or crusts of sleep in the corners of her eyes, a spray of dandruff, a breath made human by pizza and cigarettes. And there are parts of her still molten, not yet fixed, not yet womanly. She is only a little girl. Nothing like the dream-sleek maiden after all. In class she eats Mallo Cups washed down by Pepsi. And paints her fingernails blue.

By the end of the semester he cannot always remember her name.

That was not the invariable pattern, Wilkens knew. Sometimes infatuation stumbled into love, and wives were discarded and girls made wives. And sometimes the infatuations grew into little earthly dalliances. But mainly the sexual impulsiveness was just one of the small, quiet, abrasive elements in the professorial life, a slight infection one always ran a risk of, just as doctors ran comparable risks in the wards.

Wilkens now was locked into something other than any of these, and so old resolutions were not available to him. He knew that Fay Lester would not pass away into chimera, as others had. Certainly he did not want to leave his wife, not even for a moment. And he did not want to have an affair, a complicating and difficult liaison. What he wanted was for all this Fay Lester business to go away and let him be, for her to get out of his body and his mind so that he could get back to the trim arrangement of his life, so that he could have back his time and energy to go on compiling the little notes and gentle observations about literature which he had used, like currency, to buy his existence.

He did not need Fay Lester and he did not want her. He was even angry that she had come upon him this way, unbidden, unexplained. But where could he direct his anger? Nor could he be free of this passion, which was larger than desire, by a simple act of will. Even if he had had such a will. He thought back to the golden high school cheerleader. Even now, across the decades, the throb of that recalled madness drummed in him a bruising tattoo. And surprised him.

So here I am again, he thought, half a lifetime later. GO DONNE GO! HIP HIP FOR HERBERT! C-R-U-S-H CRASHAW! TRAMPLE TRAHERNE! Fay Lester, my metaphysical cheerleader. Wilkens groaned at the bitter portents in the bone. You cannot fight with flesh.

Outside, across the darkness, the lights of Cobbton twinkled as in a fairytale village. He distinguished the lights in Neil's high turreted room, burning bright, like a beacon.

"Look at him. Look at that ox," Uncle Norman said, grabbing Neil in a great hug.

Norman Wilkens, three years younger than his brother, had come from Elmira for Thanksgiving, with his bouncy wife Elaine and their three children: Stephanie, at fifteen, nearly passed beyond earliest angular adolescence to the edges of a comely young womanhood; Joseph, Peter's age; and Fred, at ten, the baby.

Norman took Neil by the shoulders and held him away like a sweater.

"Just look at him, will you. He's grown a foot at least." And then, elaborately, looking all around, "So where is she? Thanksgiving and you didn't invite your girlfriend over to meet us? What's the matter? You're ashamed? Or maybe you couldn't decide which one to bring, huh? Is that it? Tough luck, Steph," he shouted over to his daughter, who watched him with practiced blankness, determined to be inured to her outrageous father. "I can see this Adonis is up to here with the girls."

Neil shuddered that his uncle would suddenly, characteristically, show them all where he thought "here" was. But Norman pulled him back into his arms again and squeezed, then let him be, going on now to Peter in his exuberant ceremony of love and greeting.

Neil stood his ground, but his father watched him visibly writhing, the boy impaled now upon a sensitivity to his sex so exquisite that he could bear nothing public about it, like a sufferer from one of those rare diseases in which any sunlight at all can scorch and blister the skin. It would take more than Uncle Norman's jostling affection and the kidding about his girls to make him bolt out of a room, a house, his skin. But not much more.

And so it went—Norman Wilkens in an endless touching and bustling in and about the children, them, and the past year's events; Elaine dissolving into the kitchen with Mildred; the younger boys rattling in and out of everything; Stephanie with a book in the bay window of the den, doomed to these two days. Neil was nowhere.

At four, colleagues appeared for a couple of hours of easy drinks. Then they left. And then the ritual of the feast took them into the evening and into the profound structures that arranged them happily.

The next day, from mid-morning to mid-afternoon, the day bright and November-mild enough to walk in, they visited teaching friends who lived on a farm twenty miles from Cobbton. Others visited too, arriving and leaving constantly, making a circuit of the genuine barnyard, standing by the edge of the large fireplace, drinking a warm punch, admiring the mountains already capped with a dusting of early snow. They talked about books, projects, vacations to come, children visiting from college. This was the soft and gentle and unstressed world where he belonged and must stay. The hard wings beating and flickering at his existence for the past two months must be stilled, driven off. *Must* be. Here, in the midst of his central pleasures, he would find the talisman and the strength to do it. He could tell. Already it was easier.

The youngest Wilkens children roamed the farm, its fields and woodlot and stream, from time to time returning, brambly and muddied, to report whatever they could remember to bring back. Stephanie and Neil stayed as far from each other as from their parents, circling like satellite moons but bent on a comet's course, waiting for gravity to lessen and the great chance to speed into their expanding universe, to rush into and after it before it got away.

When the time came for the Wilkenses to leave, the boys found Stephanie gazing by the side of the stream, Neil in the barn's private loft.

At three, Thomas Wilkens took his brother to his health club in the Y. He lent him equipment and they played briefly at handball.

"At our age, this is the stuff that kills you, you know," Norman said, stripping off his sweat-sodden clothes.

"I work out three times a week. I ride a bike or walk almost every day. My weight is perfect." Thomas Wilkens slapped his reasonably flat belly. "Hell, there are guys my age playing pro football." He walked into the shower room.

"Yeah," his brother said after him. "Two. And five hundred more our age in coronary care units every day from handball or something like it."

After the shower they sat in the steam room, then showered again and sat in the dry heat of the sauna.

"If handball kills, this saves," Norman said, resting back against the redwood walls, his eyes closed as the heat unraveled his muscles, fiber by fiber. "This is glorious. I've got to do something like this. I should take the time. I should force myself. I'm forty-one, Tommy."

"You make it sound like a terminal disease."

"So? Isn't it?"

"What's the matter, Norman? Have you got trouble?"

"No. I don't think so. Nothing I can name, anyway, or describe." The heat pressed into his brain. "Last year, when I turned forty, I thought I was going to be depressed or something. You know? Forty? Middle aged? That? But I wasn't. It was more like a joke, everyone kidding. But it's like I must have thought, OK, forty. Enough is enough. That's it. And now I'm forty-one, sooner than I thought." He laughed. "This is very typical, isn't it?"

"Yes," his brother said. "I think so. Typical, which also means natural. A shock of recognition. But forty isn't sixty, and even sixty isn't so bad anymore I hear."

"I'm not depressed. It isn't that," Norman Wilkens said. "It's just what it obviously is." He opened his eyes and blinked the heavy sweat out of them and glanced over at his brother, the two of them alike enough in looks to be twins. "Tommy, is it tough teaching with all those girls around?"

"Not so tough," he responded quickly. He looked back at his brother. "It's not such a glamorous thing. From the outside, I know, it looks like a . . . a harem. And sure, things go on. But altogether not much. Not as much as the public likes to think. Coeds, after all, have always had a strong sexual connotation in the culture. But you get used to it. To see what they look like, many of them, at a nine o'clock class in the winter, it's not so hard to avoid temptation of either thought or deed." He was trying to inflect his voice with humor and lightness, much as he might as a lecturer.

"Were you ever tempted?"

"Yes," he said, then quickly, "Sure. More than once. But tempted more by the *idea* of something than anything else. Like an aesthetic consideration. Do you understand that, an aesthetic consideration of temptation? More interested in the mechanism of lust than in screwing? The way a theologian can explore the dazzling ramifications of divinity without actually, personally, believing in a religious God?" He was teaching now and felt safe.

He was strong and certain about everything now. His brother, their families, a Thanksgiving together, his friends and their stability—it had all been the anodyne of Order that he had needed, the modicum of ritual upon the balance beam that had brought him back to equilibrium. He inhaled deeply the superheated air of the sauna; it expanded his lungs, *him,* to a giddiness of well being. He had sweated her out of himself as easily as that. He got up. They had had enough heat.

"Sometimes I think of my daughter," Norman Wilkens confessed. "I worry about her. And what they'll think in a couple more years."

"What my Neil is thinking now?"

"Yeah. And middle-aged men."

"Sure. Right. Sometimes. But this is such a mystery? Something that never occurred to you till now?"

"No. What's new is that I think about it now at all. A lot."

"Well," Thomas Wilkens said, moving to the sauna door, tired of the conversation, of its weight, the heat sapping him now, "Let's say it's human. The human condition. It's what we're about." He left the sauna.

"Nothing else?" his brother shouted after him, but his words were quickly broken in molecules of heat.

Monday bloomed. The day itself was edged and sharp, like a newly whetted knife, and cold enough to startle but not to hurt. A good time for waking up, or for homestretch bursts at the end of the semester; or, for some, for fresh starts altogether. Wilkens resonated to the frequency of the day, and the day echoed him back.

His early classes sparkled, with him and the students thinking up to levels beyond, so that he, the teacher, could believe the previous slogging weeks had been worth it after all. In the eleven o'clock mail he received notice that an article he had worked on now and again for the past two years had been accepted for publication by the prestigious *Seventeenth-Century Studies.* The article, "Metrical Systems in Crashaw and Traherne: Catholic and Protestant Sensibilities," would be printed in thirty months. Lunch in the faculty dining room surprised them all—crisp shrimp, avocado salad. And in the afternoon student after student came well prepared to present and discuss topics for the course's major paper. By four o'clock he whooped as he soared down to home.

All day long Fay Lester had not crossed his mind. He had not even had to pretend not to be thinking of her: no more sudden looking up out of a colossal reverie; no more scurrying around the campus; no more tumbling mixture of desire and chagrin. So he was free at last, and would, in time, lean back leisurely into this aberration and consider it, recollect it in tranquility as he might recall some book or poem that had, in its progress, grasped him fiercely about the heart. He would, when the time came, consider this whole incident with meticulous and maybe even scholarly detachment and interest, measuring the larger ambiguities of life and his little adventure as best he could.

But not now. Now he was free. He let his bicycle dive through the darkening streets and whooped again, even to his own doorstep.

That night he made love to Mildred and named her again and again in his pleasure and hers, like Adam figuring it out for the first time.

He was ready for Fay Lester on Tuesday afternoon, but she did not come to class, the first time she had missed that semester. He had prepared against her, the vaccine of life's neat joys his shield; but he had not prepared for her absence, and the momentum of his defense, the anticipation of his victory over her, carried him through and beyond the resistance he had gauged for into nothing. He fell, like one of the Three Stooges who rushes to break down the door which opens at the last moment; or like Lucifer and his mighty host cast over the battlements of Heaven, falling further than time through viscous Chaos into rock-hard Hell. He could have fought *her*, but he could not vanquish the unexpected memory of her, for in memory there is substance greater than in objects, and in memory there is longing. By the end of the class he could hardly breathe, suffocating in a delirium of Fay Lester. How could this be happening? He clenched himself into a fist against his life just then, and shook himself at it.

In his own college days one Christmas vacation he went skiing in Utah, and in the middle of the second day he followed friends out onto a cornice of snow which collapsed. He never knew how far he fell, and all the time he was falling he was within snow that was falling too, that stayed tight and heavy around him. When he hit he dug straight into a snowbank and was buried. Later they told him he was only buried for five minutes, but he could never tell that from what he felt while falling and buried. He only knew that he was in terror and yet amazingly beyond time all at once. And he remembered that it was not the terror of death and dying that he felt, but the terror of hopelessness: the terror that he would *not* die, and would not change, either, out of the entombing whiteness.

That was what he felt now, in his office seated by his window, trembling, when Fay Lester knocked at his door and opened it and asked if she could enter.

"I'm sorry I missed class, but I had a lot of trouble getting back from where I was."

"That's OK."

"I was marooned. There were six of us. We spent the weekend in this guy's father's lodge in New Hampshire and we got snowed in. Which wasn't the worst of it."

"Well, I'm glad you made it back OK. I suppose you came to talk about your paper?"

"It wasn't easy. This guy was from Dartmouth and I think those guys from Dartmouth are a little crazy. Hanover is too far away from anything." He did not want to know. He did not want to hear.

"Your paper?"

"I don't know what I want to do a paper on."

"Have you thought about it?"

"To tell the truth, not much. I thought maybe something about love. They all write about love a lot. I don't know." She was swinging about, trying to hit something, obliged to go on but not much caring.

"Love in seventeenth-century poetry is a pretty broad topic, don't you think? You would have to narrow it down considerably. Religious love? Secular love? Love as a symbol? The convention of love poetry?"

"Yes."

"Yes? Yes *what*? Do you have any more specific ideas?" But what was he asking her? There was a roaring in him.

"No. I thought maybe you could make some suggestions."

"Would you rather come back another day? Think about it and then come back? You seem, well, not into the subject." He began to hit his hand on his desk softly.

"It was this weekend. You wouldn't believe it." And then Fay Lester laughed like it wasn't trouble she had had in high New Hampshire, or had brought back with her to his office. "No, Dr. Wilkens," she came back to what was at hand. "I think it would be better for you to assign me something to write about. It's late, only three weeks left in the semester. I'd learn more if you'd just tell me what to look for and I got right down to doing it."

"But selecting a topic is supposed to be part of the learning process. What you select helps me to understand what you've learned." He waited for her response, but she sat still, watching him. And then he wanted her to see deeply enough, wanted her to see his anger and to understand it, as if by her knowing she would withdraw from his life and leave him to return to peace. But what could he expect? That she could in some way *quench* herself? Cease in her nature? Get to a nunnery? He expected nothing; he hoped.

"You could write on *carpe diem.* You remember that, don't you? My lecture?" She nodded. "That would keep you away from Crashaw and Traherne. You'd like to stay away from them, wouldn't you?" She nodded again. She opened her notebook and prepared to take notes. "You'd get to read and think about some good stuff. Remember Herrick, 'To the Virgins, to Make Much of Time'—'Gather ye rosebuds while ye may,/Old Time is still a-flying'? Remember that? Or 'Corinna's Going A-Maying'—'Come, let us go, while we are in our prime,/And take the harmless folly of the time!' And Waller's magnificent 'Go, Lovely Rose'? And, of course, Marvell's 'To His Coy Mistress.' Did you read all those poems, Miss Lester? They were on the syllabus, as well as others." He stood up and walked around the desk. He could sit no longer, as if he could not willingly go over his precipice in a padded office chair. "Do you know what *carpe diem* is about, Miss Lester?" He listened to the anger, the accusation, in his voice, the snarl in it.

"Yes," she pushed back against what she heard, the anger. And more.

"What?" He thought he was shouting. Would Billings in the next office hear him?

"*Sex,*" she told him, almost ready to stand herself.

"*Death,*" he corrected her, nearly a shriek.

"*What's wrong with you?*" she shouted. And then she did stand up to face him.

"You don't want to write this paper, do you?"

"NO. I DON'T. But I've got to, don't I?"

He turned away and walked back to his desk.

They both sat down. He turned in his chair more than sideways from her. He looked obliquely out toward Cobbton. The concluding line to Herrick's trivial tinkling couplet clanged in him like a curfew knell: the folly of the time, the folly of the time.

The folly of time.

At last he heard her gently say, as if she had been talking to him but he had not heard,

"But I *don't* have to write this paper, do I?"

He said nothing for as long as he could continue to believe that he was going to answer her question as he had always thought he would answer such questions, and when he gave that up he stepped into space and said,

"Perhaps not."

He waited for the room and then the building and then his life to crack into pieces. For Billings listening in the next office to come running out, denouncing him to the faculty as a hypocrite and a liar, for the atoms of what he had always said and believed about life's moral necessities and balances to coalesce into a fissionable mass of personal holocaust. But he was elated instead, and stunned to discover that he was elated. "Perhaps not," he repeated, and turned to look at her. The beauty and allure that had to this moment astonished him now reached out more like the soft promise it was, and maybe always had been.

"What do I say now?" he asked her. "What do I say next?" Having gone so far toward his perdition, he could be whimsical, like Hamlet, clowning by the graveside, clarified by what he had already dared even though trapped into a strict course. So are mountaineers sometimes elated and eased upon attaining a desperate ledge where they can rest and recoup, but from which they cannot descend. It isn't the way they want to go; it is the only way left.

But of course Wilkens still had options, if he chose.

"I have a friend who has an apartment I can get," Fay Lester said, taking his options away. "Listen, let me handle this. I guess you've got to be careful."

He wondered if she mocked him. But no; her experience with Dimitri Varnov must have schooled her. Certainly it must have been the impetuous Russian and not this efficient girl who had disvalued the world's opinion, to his own loss. Fay Lester knew, kindly and firmly, what she was about. Increasingly he was charmed by precisely what was happening, more than he was excited by what would happen.

And so it was arranged. On the Friday after this coming Friday, he would go to an address in Cobbton village which she gave him. At three in the afternoon. It was reasonably safe.

Standing by the office door she said, "Dr. Wilkens, you don't know what a load off my mind this is."

So it could not be his desire for her that compelled him. Not now.

When we set off across a chartless sea toward a landfall we can only dimly surmise—and even that doubtfully, as in a dreamscape where there is no part we can count on; only at best a far shore and the oceanic sweep—then every act becomes a tactic, a response to the universe. We sail *when* we have wind, we sail *where* there is leeway. We dodge squalls and run in troughs of heavy seas; staying afloat and heading into the western airs is all that matters. So Wilkens sailed through his week-and-a-half voyage, uncertain where he was taking himself or why, but certain that he was in motion again, no longer trapped in the mad latitudes of the past few months. And that seemed enough. He had the order he had wanted to wrest from Fay Lester, now that he had made his pact. His life was less feverish again. There might be shoals out there awaiting him, but he commanded his own ship. He was vibrant with perception, keen with curious insight, as long as he kept moving, an actor, a participant. Only when he sometimes thought to call it off would the old leering panic and confusion start to throb in his body. Committed, he was safe. If that was the price he had to pay, then he could.

He met his classes and his students in conferences, worked on faculty committee assignments, wrote on his review of a book for *Renaissance Studies*, played handball at the Y, drove with Peter to the high school basketball game at Marlton, dined with Mildred on Saturday at the Brookshires, spent Sunday happily with the *Times*. The week was firm. Even when Fay Lester came into class he did not falter. Instead he considered (and with odd pleasure in the belittling irony) that what had seduced him was an idea after all, and not passion itself; it was a fate not unfit for a scholar/acolyte of the ghostly poet Traherne, who had of his own human predicament written:

> I knew not that there was a Serpents Sting,
> Whose Poyson shed
> On Men, did overspread
> The World: not did I dream of such a Thing
> As Sin; in which Mankind lay Dead.

And then it was Friday, and time. He showered thoroughly and dressed with special care—new undershorts and T-shirt, no holes in his socks—ate his usual thin breakfast and then went about his day, as ordinary a Friday as he had ever spent. At one-thirty he returned home. Mildred, an audiologist, was somewhere out in the country testing grade schoolers for hearing difficulties. For an hour he sat in his study, his mind traveling around and around the edges of a contemplation.

He did not want Fay Lester; his blood did not rage for her as it had in the earlier months of the college year, as years ago it had raged for his golden cheerleader. He had never made great sexual demands upon his life, nor had Mildred; they had been on that point, as on most others, satisfied and well mated. What he wanted from Fay Lester, he decided over and over again as he circled about in the vagaries of such measuring, what he wanted was to do what he was going to do, to do this outrageous and nearly irrational thing. It was all as simple and as complex as that. He looked at his walls; four hundred square feet of books, he had once calculated. And so had all their knowledge come to this.

At two-thirty he started off. He walked down to the denser part of the village. The day was cold but not hard, clear but not gleaming as winter days could be in January, after snowstorms in the reflecting sun. This was early December, that time of year without equilibrium, when days as late as autumn can come back or overnight deep winter can burst like a bomb. He turned left at Lamont Street, the nearest Cobbton could come to a "quarter": three blocks of closer houses which had been converted into apartments. Some young faculty lived in this area, and students from the college who, in their senior year, could live off campus if they wanted; and people between college and whatever was to come afterward lived there; and single workers in the marble quarries twenty miles away; and older pensioners. An art gallery, two bars, a bookstore, some lunchrooms and assorted shops.

Wilkens had been into the area often enough. It would not appear unusual for him to be there now. He walked up the wide wooden stairs at 327 Lamont Street, into the foyer, up to the second floor landing and, as she had directed him, immediately into the front apartment.

She sat deep in a very old high-backed overstuffed reading chair, her legs tucked beneath her, her long golden-white hair a mantle, the light from the window sculpting the high, tight curve of her breasts. If he had not come here under the lash of appetite, looking at her now he wished he had. All about there softly played a folk-rock song about mountains and trees.

"Hi," she said, getting up. "You're right on time. Did you find this place OK?"

"Yes." He took off his muffler, gloves, overcoat and dropped them on the arm of a sofa. He looked around at the apartment, but he could not tell from what he saw who might live here, who Fay Lester's friend was, someone like him more permanently based, or perhaps just a student like her. And waiting in the closet to charge out with a camera when they were in each other's arms? Were there tape recorders scattered about? Old jealous boyfriends lurking (Dimitri Varnov)?

But Wilkens had dealt with his apprehensions over the past ten days, and he had learned not to think about what would happen and what he would do if caught. There was too much he could terrify himself with that way, and no solution either. Once he stopped thinking of catastrophe, the dread of anticipation nearly went away. What he was left with was the proper view: he was taking a chance, but not so great a one. And that, more than her, was what he wanted.

In the middle of the room they stood looking at each other. Had he expected her to talk? What *had* he expected from her? Or from himself? That he would amuse her with witty discourse? My vegetable love should grow/Vaster than empires and more slow?

"Well," she said, "let's go." She walked into the bedroom.

She stripped quickly and stood naked across from him before he had gotten out of his shoes and socks.

"I thought you might want to look at me."

He worked at his clothes more quickly. And then he was naked with her. They got into the bed together and he enwrapped her and began to kiss her. She reached down between them and took him into her hand. Her hand was ice. After a time he rose above her. Before he entered her she said,

"Listen. I don't have to take the final exam either, do I?"

"No," he said. "No." And down he went.

He walked back from the village to the campus, nearly three miles. All the way he waited for his thoughts, but the heavy words like "adultery" did not come. Nothing did, neither *tristesse* nor guilt nor exuberance nor gaiety. If he felt anything to which he could give a name, it would be accomplishment, achievement, but not as in a triumph. All he could compare it to was how he felt when his article had been accepted for publication by *Seventeenth-Century Studies*. Then and now his life seemed stronger, better balanced, affirmed, prospective, as if it was running on, evenly, well tuned, which was all life was supposed to do.

In his office, between the writing of one letter to a friend and the writing of another, the actual statement "contented with life" occurred to him. What a minimal way of expressing what that means, he thought. But then he was no poet, nor was he meant to be. He was, rather, an attendant to events. At five-fifteen he started home.

Parked in front of his house was a state police car. He ran into the house. A trooper, large and gray, was speaking to Mildred. Whatever he had said to her she had not comprehended yet. Even as Wilkens rushed to her, he saw her absorb the statement like a branch recoiling in a terrible wind.

"No," she said. "Oh no." She did not see her husband next to her. She was sliding quickly into shock.

"That is the charge, Ma'am. Would you please call him?" The trooper was gentle.

"What? What is it?" Wilkens demanded.

"I have a warrant for the arrest of Neil Wilkens on the complaint of Cecily Grant and her father, Frederick Grant," the trooper opened his paper and began to read from it, "who alleges that on December the . . ."

"What?" Wilkens broke in. "Tell me what?"

"Rape," the trooper said, lowering the paper. What could the details mean now? "In the first degree. If your son is at home, would you please call him?" Mildred's hands were knotted into her hair; she was frozen between ripping and screaming. Peter stood, had been standing, halfway up the stairs.

"Is Neil home?" Wilkens asked his second son, who nodded, wide with fear. "I'll get him," he said to the trooper. "Let me get him. There will be no trouble. Just let me get him," as if he imagined violence. He ran quickly to the stairs and up them to the high dark turret. The door was open.

"Neil?" He turned on the light and looked about. The boy lay on his bed. "Neil, there's a state trooper downstairs who has a warrant . . ."

"I heard," the boy said. "It's a lie."

"You'll tell me about it, but right now we have to go down and go with the trooper. Now listen to me, Neil. *Neil, sit up.*" The boy rose slowly.

"She's a goddamn liar," he said.

"Good. Fine. Just listen to me. Don't talk to the police about this, do you hear? We'll go down and you'll get arraigned and I'll get a lawyer and bail and you'll be home in an hour. Then we'll talk, OK? Neil, are you listening? For christsake, Neil, *are you listening?*"

"Yes."

Downstairs the trooper had led Mildred to a chair. Wilkens phoned Jean Lipson, their nearest friend, and told her enough to get her over to the house to stay with Mildred until he could return.

"Pete," his father said to him at the door. "Go sit by your mother. Hold her hand." By the curb, as he and Neil got into the back of the police cruiser, a cage, he knew how much of Cobbton must already be reporting this. They drove off slowly, with no siren or whirling lights.

Neil was not arraigned. In an hour the charges had been dropped.

During that afternoon Neil and three of his friends went with Cecily Grant and one by one did with her what half of Cobbton's high school males had. What Frederick Grant had discovererd that afternoon was not the act, but the size of it; he may have known even before, but only now could he abide his daughter no longer. He called the cops as much to stop her as to stop the boys of Cobbton whom she had helped along their way.

In the substation officials bustled around Frederick Grant. From time to time his rage and confusion fumed up. Wilkens and the three other fathers sat together silently on a bench across the room. The high school principal, two guidance counselors, and the school psychologist appeared, nodded at the four fathers, and went to talk to Grant. Policemen, lawyers, even a clergyman none of them knew. At last Grant relented. His daughter had more to lose (of what was left) than to gain in proceeding with the action. He put on his coat. Before he left the station he passed the four fathers and paused and looked at them. Whatever anger he had had was gone. They were all in this together. Daughters, fathers, sons.

It was difficult for Wilkens to comprehend that, little more than an hour later than usual, the four of them were eating supper together as if the last hours had only been a gimmicky technical device in a manneristic French film where the real is definable only in flickering glimpses of its underside, the way photographic negatives become positives when held at the proper angle to light. Wilkens had immediately called Mildred to tell her that Neil was safe, that it was all over. They were coming home. He would stop on the way for a bucket of fried chicken. "Make a salad," he told her. "And make me a very large martini." Mildred had broken into laughter and tears. By the time they got home she would be solid again.

Was this a celebration, he wondered at the table? Should he open champagne and make a playful toast? It was not the kind of victory you crow about, exactly. Or do you? Wilkens considered his son. There was no repentance in him. Or embarrassment. He had undergone his rite of passage and survived it, more narrowly than most. But if his danger had turned out to be greater, so too would be his reward tomorrow, when he and the feral pack he roamed with would howl his praises.

The telephone rang frequently throughout the evening, and he and Mildred took turns delicately explaining to their friends what had happened. To every single one's amusement.

He could not fall asleep at once that night. The day hovered over him; it had been such a day. He tried to make distinctions, to force these rare events into an insight or a judgment, to make something out of these prodigies. But it all blurred, collapsed as if he were building with soft concrete where he needed brick. His last thought before sleep finally came was that there was perhaps nothing special to be understood; that nothing extraordinary had happened. Only that it had happened to him. That time and chance happeneth to all men.

Monday began the week of final exams and the windstorm of term papers, excuses, pleas for incomplete grades and all the other crises that the young can invent for themselves. But the true weather held good. Wilkens rode his bicycle to school and waded into the last high tide of the semester.

Tuesday afternoon he gave the final exam in the seventeenth-century course and collected the term papers. He announced,

"I'll read the papers and grade the exams and you can pick them both up from me next semester. If you want your final grade as soon as possible, give me a stamped, self-addressed postcard." And then he set them to scribbling.

Fay Lester was in the classroom. She wore the same sweater and skirt that she had worn on Friday. To remind him? She bent to apparent work over a bluebook and turned it in with the rest of the class. She left no term paper, but no one noticed or would have.

After class, in his office, he went through the pile of exams until he came to hers. He opened it. It was blank. Inside was a postcard addressed to her at her home somewhere on Long Island.

Through the rest of the week he read exams and term papers and dutifully wrote comments between the lines and in the margins, and a concluding paragraph or two at the end. He held no great illusions about what was accomplished by his responding in this reasonably labored detail; few students considered what he said in any significant depth. The grade at the end of the comment loomed too large. But he felt responsible to his function, and to his own knowledge. He would do his part, let them make of it what they may.

Monday again. The campus was mostly empty, all but a few students gone for their long Christmas vacation. Wilkens settled in, after the cushion of the weekend, to deciding final grades. After lunch that day he got to the seventeenth century. In his grade book, by Fay Lester's name, there was a C for her midterm exam. In the column for the term paper he wrote "accepted." For the final exam he put a noncommittal check, to keep the record straight at least. For the final grade he put a C. He marked her postcard and mailed it along with all the others late that afternoon. He signed the grade sheets for his classes and turned them in to the registrar. And that was the end of that.

For the rest of the week he arranged his files, began to look over his lecture notes for the courses he would teach next semester, and worked on his review article. It was a gentle time, one of the periods in the academic year which he enjoyed most, like a deep breath, like time out in a game. That Friday afternoon they would drive down to New York to visit for a week with their oldest friends, a couple who went back to their own graduate school days. It was a week they all gave each other every year, like a gift —a time for absorbing the city, for shows, restaurants, shopping, bookstores, and long evenings of talk. It was a good week right now for Wilkens to look forward to, light and buoying as he knew it would be.

Not that he was sinking. His days and nights fit well enough to suit him. Fay Lester had not seeped through unexpected fissures in his soul to poison his dreams. His life was as abundant as he could want it to be, and as much more of his life as he had had already stretched out before him, waiting. But he could not place what he had done in a sufficient context. The act had settled so much that was turbulent, yet did not feel completed. He had explained himself to himself in every way, and every way was right but not *enough*—as if he would pour a cup of water into a bucket and the level would rise with every cup, but the bucket would never be full.

What most disturbed him was the recurrence of the memory of falling through the cornice of snow and being buried. He would think about Fay Lester in controlled and rational terms, like the exegesis of a poem; but then, unbidden, would come the memory of that nearly fatal accident so long ago. After a few moments he could drive the memory away, but he could not stop it from arriving when it chose. Twice now in four months his mind determined him against his conscious will: first his virulent agony for Fay Lester, and now this memory. He looked forward to his New York visit, which would scrub all of this away.

Fay Lester stood in the opened door of his office.

"You son of a bitch," she screamed. He turned into air, his atoms spinning off in all directions. He could feel each of them go. "You rotten miserable son of a bitch."

"Close the door," he managed. But she did not.

"A *C.* You gave me a *C.* My mother told me on the phone."

"Please. Close the door." She could not hear him; her anger burned away everything as she advanced.

"How could you do it? A C? Listen, you. I was probably the best thing you ever had. And you . . . you stink. I'd give you an . . . F. An F *minus*!" He got his body together and stumbled from behind his desk to the door, to get it closed just before she said, "What are you trying to do, blackmail me? Extort me? A C for a lay? What next? A B for going down on you? Jesus, what do I have to do for an A, tricks?" She wept as only rage can weep.

"I wasn't grading you," he tried to explain, his throat so suddenly constricted that it was raw. "I didn't think you cared about the grade. I was trying to be safe, to avoid suspicion. You can understand that, can't you?" He wanted to touch her shoulder, to soothe her, but he did not dare. "Suppose someone who worked for an A found out that you got an A? What would happen?"

"What do I care? What difference is that to me? And let me remind you, Dr. Wilkens, I *did* work for my grade. You didn't talk about different work when you made the deal." She wept harder yet. "You son of a bitch."

"Please," he said. "Don't take it personally. I wanted to protect both of us. I didn't want to take a chance."

"But you *did.* You *did* take a chance." She raised her arms, her fists, and shook them as if he did not understand and she would batter down his ignorance.

But they meant different things.

"*Another* chance," he said. Then he added, softly, rasping, "Any *more* chances." But then he was looking somewhere else, at long vistas that had unexpectedly begun to open, at a view so vast he could have fainted from it, and over or through it all a bloom of light was rising and widening and rushing toward him, intensifying until his eyes seared. He staggered. Vaughan swept through him as what he saw must once have swept through Vaughan:

> I saw Eternity the other night
> Like a great Ring of pure and endless light,
>   All calm, as it was bright,

And round beneath it, Time in hours, days, years
Driv'n by the spheres
Like a vast shadow mov'd, In which the world
And all her train were hurl'd;

And then it darkened, snapped out like an electric bulb. By small but absolute degrees he let drift out of him Vaughan's hallucinated universe. In the blackness, over his heaving breath, he heard her say, "Then you won't do it?" She had sobbed down.

"Do what?" She sounded distant, far away, as if his eardrums had been pressured, muffled. The darkness changed into a dull, unilluminated whiteness like the inside of a cloud. "Do what?" he repeated.

"Change my grade?"

Her grade? "I can't," he said. "I . . ." He could not keep a steady train of thought. "I'd have to write a reason for the registrar." The soft white helpless dream of the snow packed in around him, blurring everything. "It would—could—draw attention . . ." He stopped. What difference did explanations make now? What explanations were there? "No. I'm sorry. I can't."

"You could," she flared up again a little. "You could. You're just afraid."

"Yes," he said, "I am."

When she was gone he sat quite still and let the first terror she had brought in with her subside. He let fade the jagged collage of public accusation and denial that had first sprung through him, the tumult of fear that he would lose . . . what? Everything? But what could that mean? No. The loss he had sustained would be a small one, something he would hardly notice in his life as it had been and would be lived hereafter. There would be no more chances.

At last he was empty.

Tomorrow they would drive down to the city. That evening, the reservations already made, they would eat at Chez Victor on 53rd Street. Vichyssoise, artichokes vinaigrette, escargot, coq au vin, a 1969 St. Julien. A supper you could count on.

Surviving Adverse Seasons

> The Universe is either a chaos of involution
> and dispersion, or a unity of order and providence.
> If the first be truth, why should I desire to linger in the
> midst of chance, conglomeration, and confusion?
>
> —Marcus Aurelius Antoninus

Britannia est insula.

So it began, again, for Abel Harnack. Another beginning in a life, lengthening, of many beginnings. And now a few endings. One at least.

Britannia est magna insula.

"And now, so that you will learn to hear as well as see the language, so that you will *feel* the beauty of it in the mouth, will you please read aloud? Will you," she glanced down at her class list, "Mr. Harnack, begin for us."

He read clearly and accurately the two lines and then the two lines following them to the end of the paragraph. *Britannia est patria nostra, sed Britannia est terra pulchra.*

It had taken him a year to get here, this far. Monday evening. Page one. *Britannia est insula.* But even that morning he had not been certain that he would do it. He had not felt compelled into it as, in the past, he always had been—urgent, hungry, charging into endeavor, racing after accomplishment. Now he did not feel that way at all.

"Go on," his daughter had said to him at breakfast. "Do it." He did not live with Vivian, but after her husband, Charles, had driven off to his work and the two children had left for school, he would come often to eat a later breakfast with her. Unless she had something else to do that took her away. Then he would walk on past her house and into the city and into whatever vagaries his life just then, that day, would tilt him toward.

He might conclude upon a group of workmen breaking a street apart to fix a sewage pipe. He would drift down the street to them like a heavy log in a slow stream and go aground upon them, caught in their activity, the shattered air, the blasting of the pummeling jackhammer, the sputtering of the blue arcwelder, the revving up and down of the gasoline engine generator.

They would all subside at lunchtime and he would drift on, free. Perhaps to spiral through department stores, sometimes to visit factories and small machine shops he had once known well. Through the summer past he had watched young men play baseball in all the city's parks. And in the evening he would walk home, past his daughter's house (though at least once a week to supper there) to his own house and to his evening in which he would do whatever occurred to him, unless nothing did.

At twelve or a little before, he would drink a small glass of Scotch whiskey and then go to a thorough sleep, unprovoked by fears or passions or expectations. And at six he would awake.

"Go on," his daughter Vivian said to him at breakfast. "Do it. Go on and do it. It will do you good."

"Good? Good for what?" he asked her.

"Oh come on, Dad," she said, turning from the sink and their dishes. She said no more. That was as far as they ever got upon that point any longer.

"Very good, Mr. Harnack," Sylvia Warren said to him. "Thank you. Now Mrs.? . . . Miss Green, will you take it from there?" Miss Green took it from there, from Britannia through Europa to Sardinia, to Italia, some being insula, some not, some being magna, some parva.

At the end of the two hours, at the end of the first and second conjugations and the first declension and warnings about the ablative case, Abel Harnack decided not to return the coming Monday.

"*Vale,*" Sylvia Warren said to them as they all gathered up their books.

"*Vale,*" they answered back.

Outside, in the parking lot behind the high school, the group of them broke off to their own cars, except Abel Harnack, who would walk.

"Do you want a ride?" she called to him when she saw him, alone, crossing the asphalt parking lot to Wilson Street.

"Is that your car?" he asked, walking back to her, although it clearly was her car, the small door to it already opened, her briefcase already dropped into the catchall area behind the seat.

"Yes. My joy." The car was an earlier model MG, the classic squarish roadster with narrow, wire-spoked wheels and headlights separated from the fenders, with a windshield that folded down, a walnut steering wheel, leather upholstery, the car a gleamingly waxed deep green. It was not the car he would have imagined her to drive.

But she was thin, lithe enough for it, her motions strong and quick. Nimble, he thought. And although she was gray, she wore her hair modishly straight and long, out like a helmet, square across her forehead and to an inch over her shoulders. And she smiled like the young, easily and without complication and at everything. Perhaps her car suited her after all, even if she must be, Abel Harnack guessed, fifty-five or more.

"That's a fine-looking car." They both waited beside it. "OK," he said. "But I don't live far. Only down Wilson Street about a half a mile." He went to the other side of the car. "How do I get in?"

"Like this. You sit in first and then swing your legs in." She did it. He opened his door and followed her example. "Fine. You did that just fine."

"I learn things quickly."

"I noticed that in class." The car burst to life. She backed up and then drove across and out of the lot, turning left on Wilson Street at his direction. She drove gracefully, snapping the gearshift through its pattern, pushing the car a little quickly, but well controlled. She drove with pleasure, Abel Harnack thought.

In two minutes she stopped before his house, where he had pointed it out, the motor running. He swung himself out of the car.

"Thanks."

"It's nothing." She shifted and started off slowly. "See you next Monday." Between gears she waved her free hand. "*Vale,*" she shouted back over her exhaust.

"*Vale,*" he said softly.

Latona est irata quod agricolae sunt in aqua.

"Now here, you see," she said, "*quod agricolae sunt in aqua* is the dependent clause. It depends upon *irata* for its full meaning."

He had come back.

After the first class, at breakfast Tuesday, he had told Vivian that he probably would not go to the Latin class again; but when she asked him why, he could not say, except to say that he was not so interested in Latin as he thought he might have been and that, after all, it was not something he had been strongly decided for in the first place. He had gone and he had seen and that was that.

Vivian, sitting across from him, shrugged. After a year of trying, of anxiety and duty, she would have to go along now with him as he was. He was sixty, voluntarily retired for a year now, ever since his wife, Estelle, had died, in one week, in a wretched spasm of sudden dying for which you cannot prepare, and from which you cannot recover.

Abel Harnack buried his wife and then stopped. That was the only word for it, as if to permit himself to do anything at all again would be to accept again the world—his life, the possibility of life—as it had been. And that he would not do. He had too much decency for that, and besides, he learned things quickly. And what he had learned—quickly, in a week—was that all the assumptions of his life had been unquestioned, had simply been assumed the way a child assumes the universe: *post hoc, ergo propter hoc.* But what he had learned was that nothing did or *did not* follow from anything at all. Not the seasons, not the tides, and least of all even the smallest aspirations of man.

So for a year now he had sat out, finally neither in anger nor in contemplation. He would not get caught by the old—by any—assumptions again.

"And for next week I want you to review all we've learned about first- and second-declension nouns and to study the declension of *bonus* in all its genders. And I want you to read and translate the first three stories in Appendix A, which begins on page 280. Write out your translations, and remember, think of the principles involved."

After class, in the parking lot, he told her he would not be coming back to class.

"But why? You do so well. I'm surprised. You seemed to be enjoying yourself."

"*Bonus, bona, bonum?*" he asked her. "*Midas in magna regia habitabat*? I already know the story of King Midas."

"But this is just the start, just the beginning. Surely you understand that Latin isn't declensions. It's Vergil and Horace and Ovid. It's Catullus.

Vivamus, mea Lesbia, atque amemus,
rumoresque senum seneriorum
omnes uninus aestimemus assis.
Soles occidere et redire possunt:
nobis cum semel occidit breuis lux,
nox est perpetua una dormienda.

Do you know what that says?

Come, Lesbia, let us live and love,
nor give a damn what sour old men say.
The sun that sets may rise again
but when our light has sunk into the earth,
it is gone forever.

Oh, no, Mr. Harnack. Declensions and exercises are just the beginning. The end is poetry."

Beginnings again.

It was the first week of October but summery yet. The lights defining the parking lot flickered through the still heavy pulsing screen of attracted insects, like candles wavering in a slight breeze. The sound of Catullus lingered as if reverberating back from the night around them. Had she spoken, declaimed, so loudly? Were neighbors sitting now on darkened porches across Wilson Street listening to this woman cast Latin poetry at him, themselves listening to it hovering in the evening air? But of beginnings he had had enough.

"It's too far between King Midas and . . . and what you recited."

"Too far?"

"Too long. For me. I haven't time. I'm not so young a man."

"Perhaps it takes less time than you think. Have you ever studied a language before?"

"French. In high school. And for two years in college. I remember nothing of it."

"Perhaps you do. Perhaps you unconsciously remember much in your past that you think you've forgotten. It's all there, you know. The past."

He said nothing.

"Well, come on. Let me give you a ride home." She walked away from where they were standing and to her car. He did not follow.

"It's a nice night, thank you. I think I'll walk," he called over to her softly. He did not like this openness, Catullus blatant in the wide night, the talk of endings, of pasts and possibilities for all, for the air itself, to know.

"Oh come on, Mr. Harnack. I've lost students before. I don't take it personally. Don't you. Latin's not for everyone. Come on." She got into the car and waited. He came over quickly and got in. To be gone and done.

In front of his house she stopped and he got out.

"Thank you," he said.

"I hope you'll reconsider," Sylvia Warren said and waved and drove off.

He continued with Latin, although he did not reconsider. It was his determination now, after a year, not to reconsider anything. He returned on the following Monday, his lessons prepared, his exercises neatly typed. He returned as if the effort of halting the small momentum of going on, slight as it was, would require of him energies he did not wish ever to use again. Now, after a year, he had started something about which he could not care, something about which there could be no purpose, no meaning or accountability. Above all, he would—must—avoid the traps of purpose. Latin was what he had come up with, an act too remote from him to count at all; an act that could not, would never, matter to him in the years, perhaps the decades, left. He did not particularly enjoy the Latin, but he would do it and he would not think about doing it again.

During the class the rain that had gone on all day thickened, drove down like a summer storm improbably late even for the warm October they had been having.

"*Cadens imber mari similis est*: the rain falls like the sea," she had stopped the class to say, gesturing at the windows. The rain came now in sheets so dense that the wind slapped them against the building, shaking it. At the end of class she called for him to come to her desk.

"I'm glad you decided to come back. Your work is really superlative." And then, "You'll certainly need a ride home on a night like this."

"I brought my car. Thank you."

She nodded and smiled and gathered up her books and papers into her briefcase, and they walked out of the room together as the janitor came in to turn out the lights after them. From the doorway to the parking lot the rain made the darkness palpable.

"It's a bad night to drive in," Abel Harnack said.

"It can't rain this hard for long," she said. "It'll taper off." The class had gathered into a tight knot at the door wedged between the two darknesses.

"Well, here goes," Sylvia Warren said. She hunched herself over, her briefcase tight to her chest, and tucked her chin and sprinted to her car. They watched her, students now to her daring, but in ten feet they could not see her, the light from the lamps around the parking lot squeezed by the viscous rain back into the quavering globes. Then the others followed, four to one car, three to another, several to another, and Abel Harnack to his.

The cars started up and eased out slowly into Wilson Street. In the instant before he drove out, through a gap in the rain he saw her car, low and dead. He circled back into the lot and drove up next to her. Then he saw that she was out of the car with the right side of the hood up. She was bent into the engine with a flashlight. Her rain hat had slipped back. He got out and walked around to her side.

"Damn thing," she said to him. The rain eased off for a moment, and then a moment more. "It's water somewhere. I'm getting shorted out, but I can't tell where. Inside the distributor probably."

"Try and start it," he told her. "I'll take a look."

After a minute or two he waved her out. "I think it's here." He pointed to an element fixed into the line leading to the coil. "This is a radio static suppressor."

"Yes, I know. I put it in."

"They're a bad business, I think." He pulled the plug apart and removed the suppressor and reconnected the heavy wires. "Try it now."

The car started at once.

"Thank you," she shouted out to him. She raced the engine, securing it, herself. "I'm sorry you got so wet. You'll have to explain it to me next week. Please, hurry in out of the rain." She pulled the door closed and turned on her driving lights. He opened the door before she could drive off.

"Wait," he said. "That connection is still too open. You might get it wet again in this weather before you got home. Stop at my house and I'll fix it right for you." He held his coat tight about his throat, but he was already wet through.

"OK."

He drove slowly, keeping her watery headlights in his mirror. He turned into his driveway and pressed a button on his dash that opened the door to the large garage. She drove in after him into the space on the left and got out of the car and shook herself like a retriever.

"Well," she said, looking about. "This is certainly more than just a place to put a car."

Abel Harnack's garage was a workshop equipped to rebuild or mend whatever was. Or to create what was not. A large metal lathe with various milling heads, drill presses, band saws and bench saws, sanding drums, levering and bending devices, compression tools, testing equipment, oxy-acetylene and electric arc welders, racks and cabinets of wrenches, tap and die pieces, hammers, chisels, hydraulic jacks, lubrication guns and nozzles, a motorized hoist that ran on an overhead metal beam. In a corner, stacked up nearly to the roof, were dozens of small drawers like those in the oldest hardware stores where one of the objects in the drawer was tacked to the front: springs, nuts, bolts, shims, washers, wires, rods, and stock until the mind could not comprehend the variety of pieces demanded by the mechanisms of manufactured life. From an overhead rack belts and hoses and rubber and plastic fittings draped down like stalactites.

And everything in perfect array, spectacular as much for that lucidity, for the enormous accomplishment of arrangement, as for the objective demonstration that there existed so many things from which to make so many things.

"Mr. Harnack, whatever do you *do*?"

He had already lifted the hood and was at work sealing the connection, remaking it, in fact. In less than five minutes he was done.

"There," he said, pointing to it. "Better than new. You won't get stuck from that again. Your next trouble is going to come from here." He pointed to the gaskets beneath the double carburetors. He could have told her more about her car, everything perhaps. But he thought that he had gone too far already. He closed the hood and looked for her. She was still turning about in the marvel of the shop.

"I've never seen anything like it. Not even pictures or anything." She was wet and shivering but did not notice, still warmed by her discovery. Her hair was shining and flattened against her head, the ridges and notches of her bone structure clear and pronounced as the cold drew her skin tight to her skull.

"Would you like a cup of coffee?"

"Yes," she said, turning to him now. "Thank you. That would be wonderful." She walked with him across the workshop to the doorway to the house. Instead of a doorknob or handle there was a square metal plate, brushed steel. She watched him run his finger in a design over the surface of the plate. The door opened. They walked into the warmer house.

"What are you, Mr. Harnack?" she asked as she followed him into the kitchen. "What magic is this?" She laughed in delight as children do at wonder, thrilled and unnerved at sorcery all at once. He had not heard her laughter before.

"Nothing," he said. "Retired." He said nothing more until he placed the coffee before her. Until then she looked about quietly at what she could see of the house from the kitchen through its two doors and over its counter into the dining room and living room. The house was as neat and clean as ice, like water poured into a mold and frozen and then left.

"My wife died about a year ago. A year last August."

"I'm sorry," Sylvia Warren said. And then there was nothing more to say, nothing more she *could* say. She understood boundaries. She bent to her coffee.

But it was not such a boundary that Abel Harnack wanted to exist within. He wanted to erect no special defense because there are no such defenses, and he wanted nothing to defend, only to avoid, like the bitterness that had at first consumed him. In the staggering weeks after Estelle's death, after drowning and drowning, he had surged into the thin air of life again. In a second life, only this time to be lived carefully balanced upon the interstices between events and attitudes, cautiously in the shifting spaces between the molecules of human concern. So he would talk to her in order *not* to care.

"I was an inventor of sorts. And a salesman."

"An inventor?" She put down her coffee cup.

"Yes. More a tinkerer, you might say. I understood how things worked and I figured out ways to make them work better. You'd be surprised. Sometimes just the slightest thickness of the metal in a gear or the gauge of a wire in a motor can make a big difference."

"I've never met an inventor before. I'm genuinely impressed. Whenever I think of an inventor I think of Thomas Edison." She raised her cup to him.

Her eyes were very young, sharp and quick, the whites blue with vigor. He did not want to look at them.

"I'm hardly an Edison," he said. "More a Mr. Fix-it. That's how I began, as a kid. By the time I started college I had a good business going, a real one. I was making enough to pay my way and then some. And it's what I came back to. Fixing things. And then small manufacturing. And then I got a little larger. And then larger. The usual story, I guess. After awhile I had become a businessman instead of a mechanic, so I sold out so I could get back to things themselves. I took a job as a special kind of salesman. I'd go into highly technical production problems and help the engineers figure out what equipment and materials they needed and where they could get it. It was a great job for me. A little bit of everything going on, but deep too, if you see what I mean. And it left me with enough time for my own projects." He told her more about the work he had done for the industries and companies great and small, and of the shape that his advice had helped to give to our material lives. He hadn't spoken so much to someone for a long time, excepting Vivian.

Sylvia Warren got up and went to the stove to make herself

another cup of coffee. As she began to pour the hot water into the cup, she stopped. "I'm sorry," she said. "How presumptuous of me. You made me feel too comfortable."

"Oh please, help yourself. Go on, go on," he motioned to her to help herself.

But it was true. He had spoken more than he had thought to. He had intended a cup of coffee's worth of civility. Now she had bound him to a cup more. A slight tremor of refusal tickled through his legs, a memory from his more recent history of agony and rage when his body crashed about inside itself out of control, his organs ripping themselves apart as directed by the hormones and enzymes of grief and confusion. But that had ended. When everything else had ended except the simplest activities of the life process, his body had come back to itself. Only sometimes, such as now, an old forgotten neuron would synapse; but it would soon subside, for there was no energy of special hope for it to subsist upon, for it to generate a potential for action. Nothing got you, nothing *either way.* In the dark night of his soul he had learned that, and it had saved him.

"Go on," he said to her. He was not a victim any longer.

She poured her coffee and came back to her seat, drier, softer, her color returning.

"How do you invent something? How do you do it? How do you think of what to invent? It seems so . . . so *mystical.*"

"Not so mystical," he said. "All you do is think about something that somebody needs. Then you figure out how to make it."

"For instance?"

"Well, take a door lock, like the one you saw. People are always buying them, more now than ever. So there is your need. Then I figured out how to make one better than the others."

"Tell me. Tell me about the lock. How does it work?"

He took some paper from a drawer in the kitchen counter and drew diagrams to explain.

"You see, the metal plate is really quite flexible even if you can't see it is. And here, in back of the plate, are thousands of tubes. By putting fluid into some of the tubes you make a design. That's the key. When you trace the same design on the metal plate you put pressure on the harder tubes which then push down here," he indicated where on the diagram, "and from then on it works like a conventional lock with tumblers that shoot a bolt."

"That's marvelous," she said. "I'll bet you make a fortune with it."

"No," he said, "The psychology of it is wrong. People want a key they can hold in their hand, even for all the trouble it gives them. And there are other problems, like in a large family with little children who couldn't learn the design. Or suppose you wanted a friend or neighbor to come in while you were away, to water the plants or feed the fish? Instead of leaving the key under the doormat, you'd have to leave a drawing of the design." They laughed together.

"Oh my," Sylvia Warren said. "How disappointing. Did you think of all that when you invented the lock?"

"Oh yes," he said, "I've had a lot of experience with that sort of thing. But I wanted to do it. It interested me. And I did get a patent out of part of it, so I might make a little money from that."

Then he told her more about inventing. About the complicated process of a patent search and other legalities and about the cost, which surprised her ("Between one or two thousand, depending upon the complexity of the thing") and about all the ways an inventor could go about trying to make while failing to make money. Then he told her about some of his successes, the little artifacts of his skill and imagination and knowledge of the world that had added up to a small place in the spectrum of invention, and to an income that had made it possible for him to stop.

"What next?" she asked at last, her own enthusiasms for such power over things taking over for him. But she had gone too far now for a certainty and could tell (though *how,* she could not tell) that for Abel Harnack his past did not predict his future. No longer. "Sorry," she said, faithful at least to her intuitions.

"What next?" He would answer her. "*Pericula belli non sunt* and the future indicative. What else?" Again they both laughed. She rose.

"You've been just splendid," she said. "About everything. The car, the coffee, everything." She slipped quickly, agile and firm, into her still damp coat. "An inventor," she said, flipping her hair over her collar. "I've never met one."

"I've never met a Latin teacher," he said.

"No comparison," she said, her mouth making a pretty gesture. "No comparison at all."

He almost said something.

She stood before the locked kitchen door.

"Open Sesame," she said to it, and flung wide her arms and waited. "I guess I didn't say it right."

"No, you didn't. Here." He reached to the side of the door and turned a switch and stepped back about six feet. "Open Sesame, or whatever your name is." The door snapped open. Sylvia Warren gave a little shriek. "It's a sound lock. Convenient in a kitchen when your hands are full."

Sylvia Warren awoke to the day bright and scoured by the cold front that had moved through quickly in the night. Autumn was firmly here now, and even some of earliest winter, though there would be weeks left to tramp about in the woods and fields. She got out of bed and showered, made her small breakfast and, over her second cup of coffee, opened her ledger to write in it and to consult the architecture of her day, of her life.

Tuesday.

She would spend most of that morning correcting and commenting on the papers from her Latin class and then preparing for the following Monday. In the time left in the morning she would answer letters to friends, pay bills, make plans and lists. Tuesday. She would go to the Books-Sandwiched-In program at the local library, noon to one, and then on to the Triverton Nature Preserve, where she and Mildred Latham would beat through the late fields with their nets and jars for insects to bring to the Biology Club meeting that evening. At six o'clock she would eat supper with Midred Latham, as on Tuesday she always had. But before Tuesday quite began officially, she wrote about the day and the night before.

She wrote quickly and exactly, more a record than an examination of events, something like a progress report, the way building contractors complete a day with an accumulation of data about bricks laid and tons of cement poured and steel girders locked into place, or as ship captains make log entries about winds and tides and weather encountered, as if reality were only where we have been and not where we might go, or want or intend to go. When she arrived at Abel Harnack in her day, she wrote:

> Abel Harnack, late 50's (?), widower, good health, extremely knowledgeable and intelligent, fixed my car in a driving rainstorm and then later at his house. An *inventor.* His workshop a cave of magic. He is restrained? Shy? Perhaps the death of his wife only a year ago?? What does he do with himself now that he is retired? How can a man who was an inventor retire? More to be explored here.

She shut her ledger, dressed, and settled down at her desk, the exploration of the *terra incognita* of Abel Harnack put aside for now. She worked at the Latin exercises briskly. Besides pointing out what was simply incorrect in a student's work, she explained why in the margins and between the lines with little sharp indicators, her comments as much encouragement and exhortation as corrective.

Sylvia Warren had taught Latin (and some French and a little Spanish) for twenty-three years at the regional high school, with spirit and affection enough to have made the subject palatable and, finally, even attractive to those dwindling few who worked on past the grinding first year of declensions and conjugations into Caesar's *Commentaries* in the second and, ultimately, in the third year, into the sublimity of Cicero and the Poets and the difficult, silvery Tacitus. It was an odd, an anachronistic thing to do, she would herself at times consider, this teaching of smooth old Latin in a world spiky and clattering about in the exciting newness of gleaming technology and movement in space and swift-breeding opportunity. She did not defend the Latin itself—for what defense could beauty have or need? But she was not about to accept uncritically the old banners under which the Association of Classical Language Teachers marched each year in thinning ranks at the annual convention: Latin is the Language of History, or The Study of Latin Is the Best Preparation for the Study of English.

No. She could not accept that, and never had. Latin wasn't a tool. Had it been, it might have survived. Latin was its own reward; but what it could promise in that way was no longer worth enough to the young. And she could understand that. Latin was, had become, irrelevant. And Sylvia Warren along with it. Her job, not her person.

She had taught long enough to retire if she chose, though she could have stayed on at the school teaching some French and taking up other chores such as an extra study hall or two. She was fifty-three then. Her pension would be smaller than if she had taught to the end of her possibilities, and she was years away from her social security income, but she had saved enough to balance things out nicely. She could afford to leave if she wanted.

But she did not want to, not exactly. She had come to the high school when she was twenty-nine and within a year she had clicked into place like a well-hung door closing evenly. Within a year she had found the friends and interests and functions that had not changed even to this moment, that had grown larger and deeper instead, rich as wine that ages well. If satisfaction was *in itself* one of life's true joys, then in her wide contentment she was there, and shared the sentiment with Horace in the *Epistles:* "Whatever prosperous hour Providence bestows upon you, receive it with a thankful hand: and defer not the enjoyment of the comforts of life." So there were no sudden pleasures expected or gained, no longed-for excursions to exotic places or into acts that would come to her once free of her daily work. In or out of the structures of the last twenty-three years, little would change.

But she did leave the job even so, as if that step, small as it was, altering her life as little as it would, would make up the difference that she had wondered at in the smallest degrees, in the quietest of ways from the beginning: that nothing more had come about in her life than what had.

It was a curiosity to her, this lost dimension, but not a sorrow, that all her life energy and intelligence, her capacity for experience, had carried her into one experience and then another and from the fluttery and imprecise edge of each into the penumbra where an experience bordered on becoming something else, something more than the experience, fulfilling as it was, did at last become. As with her painting.

Throughout her large apartment watercolors in double-matted, deep, silver-colored frames determined nearly every wall, every room: barns, seashore villages, fishermen from riverbanks, countrysides in all their seasons. The competency of each, of the whole, burst forth in a wave of illumination that promised to come, that did not come, and the pictures fell from the near pinnacle of vision down to the flat plains of skill. This was her own estimation, staunchly held through the winds of sweeping praise her friends blew upon her at her yearly show. She did not know how to paint the explosion that she felt in herself when she would work in the rapid light, racing the sun, the shadows surely coming. But she knew enough about what she could not do to accept no man's praise as though she had.

On one wall were her photographs, compositions as logical and controlled as if she had set a huge outdoor stage with perfect sets and actors. Light and dark knew what they were doing to the people moving through their lives before her lens. But then the pictures, dried and mounted, failed to alert the viewer to the implicit dangers and predicaments of the human transactions they fixed, and instead of perception they became glances. Sylvia Warren would look at them and know that. And think that, however firm were her trills in the Mozart piano sonatas, the music fluttered but never soared. How in tennis she could never trust her second serve, as certain as it was likely to be good. Nothing, nothing at all, ever went as far as it might have. As it should.

And she had not married. Or known a man at all. And that had puzzled her more than anything else in her life. But it was not simple longing that she sat with, rarely, through a night. It was the waking urgency to truly know about those processes of life that sometimes inexplicably fail. She had always been attractive to men, and was still. If she had not courted them, neither had she built skittish barricades. At first, younger, she sought reasons in herself, like talking too much or being too enthusiastic, little alienating characteristics that she had read and heard and been warned about as a girl. But there were no reasons like that, or any others. There were no reasons at all. Sometimes people to whom something is bound by every likelihood to happen are simply missed, like the one survivor in a massive air crash or the millionth customer who stops just before he enters the store to tie his shoe and falls from Grace.

So there was nothing to reason about. She had begun as she was and nothing came along to change it. Or end it. No one, she had corrected herself. Yes, she had thought, that's right. Maybe.

She was not afraid to think about herself directly, to examine and explore the crags and crevices of herself. She had lived alone with her good mind long enough to respect it, to not be frightened of it when it was insistent. It was in *not* thinking that there was danger. That was the trouble with old maids, old maid schoolteachers, she would point out to Mildred Latham. They were afraid to think and so they acted badly, especially with men, about whom they wished to think least, tripping themselves into the safety of the dreary old flighty stereotype or bristling with hearty self-sufficiency.

She had left her job in the school because she thought then that, allowing her energies to be completely loose, perhaps they would meld together, concentrate into a creative juggernaut that would storm the battlements and . . . But nothing like that had happened. Only the old pleasures that filled her nearly to the brim.

Tuesday morning was concluded. Before she left the apartment she packed a small knapsack with the rough clothes and field boots that she would change into in the afternoon.

"Do you know how long I've looked for this, for *Vendalia tarda,*" Mildred Latham said, shaking one of the five cotton-stoppered test tubes at Sylvia Warren. "And now to find it, in *October* of all times. In a plenitude. Eggs as well." A short, heavy but soft woman, she bounced about in her kitchen like a semi-inflated beach ball, bounding off in unpredictable directions. "Just listen to this," she came back to the table. She read from a copy of *The Entomological Review* splayed across the kitchen table, supper gone awry.

> *Vendalia tarda,* although not considered a truly rare species within the Coleoptera, is yet uncommon even within its natural range, which, in the United States, is mainly southern. *V. tarda* is seldom found above the thirty-second parallel in the eastern states, the thirty-third parallel west of the Appalachians to the Rockies. It is not yet discovered in the western coastal region.
>
> The uncommonness of *V. tarda* in its own range and its only seldom and accidental appearance north of its range is accounted for by the insect's highly selective necessity for light and temperature, specific conditions which must occur not only once, but twice for the insect's passage from egg to larva to pupa to adult. This condition of quadruple diapause in *V. tarda* is nearly unique among insects. Apparently the quadruple diapause condition is continuous throughout the life cycle, and it is not unusual for four or five years to pass between the laying of the egg and the development of an adult insect able to lay another egg. And longer periods have been recorded. (Bornstein)

Mildred read more from the article and explained. "You see, the creature has to pass up through and then down through the same light/temperature ratio for each of the four stages—egg, larva, pupa, adult. It has got to be, say, thirty degrees on a twelve-hours-of-light day as the egg goes into winter, and then the same after winter as the egg moves into spring and hatches. And listen to this."

> It is unfortunate that this apparently disadvantageous life cycle limits the numerical size of the species, for *V. tarda* is

> extremely destructive of not one but five prey insects, all pests. The range of *V. tarda*'s appetite seems clearly to be a consequence of its necessity to develop in such specific stages, thus making certain that food will be available to the insect at widely divergent times within the more normal and limited insect "year."

She read on. About the difficulty of raising the insects in the laboratory because of the complex double cycles involved in the four stages.

> The length of time that would be required to work out the possible light-temperature permutations would exceed the endurance (and resources) of even the most dedicated entomologist. The very few recorded successes in the raising of *V. tarda* have been accounted for more by chance than by knowledge.

Mildred slapped her hand down on the journal page. "It's just wonderful," she said. "*Vendalia tarda.*"

"Slow to live," Sylvia Warren translated.

"Yes, 'slow to live.' " Mildred Latham stood up from the table. "I've killed and pinned six of them for tonight's meeting. A special event, you might say. And I'm taking about a dozen to Dr. Alberts at the university tomorrow. I'll drive down in the morning. Do you want to come?" She rushed on. "I'm keeping the others to see what I can do with them. And I'll check what's going on at Triverton until I can't find them any longer."

"What can you do with them?" Sylvia Warren asked. "What do you mean?"

"Breed them. Try to raise them. Take my shot at it. After all, I've never had these critters to work on. Let it be my turn to fail. Come on now, eat up. We don't want to be late for the meeting."

"Eat up what?" Within the scattered paraphernalia of their afternoon—killing jars, bottles and vials, magnifiers, aspirators, nets—here and there poked up lumps of cheese, curls of torn bread, a can of sardines, an onion started and forgotten, cups of tea gone cold.

"Yes," Mildred Latham said, "I see. I'll tell you what, old Warren. I'll buy you a hamburger later."

In the car on the way to the meeting she explained more about the problems of breeding *Vendalia tarda,* the elaborate devices she would have to imagine and build, the special habitats she must create and control, the exact regulators. "I haven't got a chance," she gaily granted. "Even if I knew just exactly what to do, I couldn't manage it for sure. I was always a field person, never good with complicated lab arrangements, and such. I've bred plenty of insects, but this is going to be something different, more exploring than doing. But what the hell." They drove on.

By the first traffic light, Sylvia Warren had decided that maybe Abel Harnack *could* manage it for sure.

Wednesday.

Wednesday was the luxury of a morning uncommitted, neither to nothing nor to something, the half-day of rest in her week, the pause for one o'clock, when she would go to the Y for an afternoon of yoga and swimming and the steam room and the dry sauna; free before Wednesday evening, when she would play piano in a trio of old friends. But at eight-thirty she called Abel Harnack and explained as best she could.

"So you see," she concluded, "what she needs is some way to make . . . to make time equal light and . . . and both to equal temperature. Sort of. But look, I'm doing a terrible job of explaining this diapause thing, and the experiment. Perhaps if you could meet Mildred Latham and have her explain the problem. I'm sure it would all be clearer than it is now."

But he said no.

Sylvia Warren recovered and apologized and said goodbye.

In the basement of Abel Harnack's house, in nearly half of it, rested a cat's cradle of various-sized wires, knitted and woven, spliced and soldered together into an intricacy too complicated for the eye to comprehend. Only at the moment it all might blur into a meaningless tangle, it did not; it held, instead, taut as sculpture, which it might have been. But it was a machine. An attempt that Abel Harnack had worked upon for years, in time he tucked in between his job and his family and his more practical devices. What he wanted to do with this machine was take an electrical charge and, by amplifying it and modulating it in exquisitely calculated increments, make the charge go on endlessly, inexhaustibly under its own power.

"It's what inventors come to sooner or later"; he tried to describe to Estelle what he was doing. "But you see," he had told her, "energy is what we are all about. From the sun to a can opener. It's what we are always working with." Estelle would nod and go on cooking. She did not understand the details of what her husband did. All she understood was him. Which had been enough for both. Still, he would tell her at length the history of the search for the grail of perpetual motion: who had tried what, and why it always failed. The mistake of the past was to use gears and levers that took as much energy to move as the energy that they would try to continue to produce. But he would not use material that way. He would use the electron's energy itself, to continue to produce itself.

A year ago he had come to where he could keep a small charge alive within his mechanism for twelve hours before his meters read out for him the slow and then quickening dissolution. On his way home from work that day he knew what he could do to gain two hours more. Even before supper he could make the modification that he had figured in and out of all through that afternoon. But when he opened his door, Estelle was gone. Vivian was there instead.

"Dad," she said. "I tried to reach you." And told him.

He had come home from work one day prepared to gain a centimeter against the universe. He found Estelle gone. She had dropped into the hospital and he had never seen her, as Estelle, again. There was nothing he could do to help her, or himself, not even the smallest thing: his voice beside her, the pressure of his hand. There was nothing he could do to help her. And if he could do nothing about that, then he would do nothing at all, ever again. He had raised his fists against the colossal outrage of the vulgarity of her dying that stripped her of the basest dignity and crushed her, smeared her like a swatted fly against a windowpane. He shrieked against the badly designed and uncorrectable device called life. And then held still, free now forever from the obscenity of creation.

In class Sylvia Warren said, "But enough of the difficulties of the imperfect indicative. Let's spend our remaining time with some poetry." For over an hour and a half she had gone over last week's exercises, through the new lessons, and then had prepared them for the work they would do in the week coming. "Now just sit back and listen to this. Don't worry about understanding it. You probably won't understand it except for a word or a phrase here or there. Just try to get the sound into your head. Each week we'll do a little more of this and you'll be surprised how much it will help you. And what pleasure it will come to be." She read to them from the *Aeneid* and then translated.

"And now, *molliter cubes.* Good night," she said to them.

"Good night. *Vale,*" the class said back. Then rose and, piece by piece, left.

"Mr. Harnack," she said to him as he passed her desk. He stopped and turned to her. "I'm sorry about the other morning. That was presumptuous of me. *Mea culpa,*" she smiled, open, clean. "I certainly must appear to be a presumptuous person to you, though I am not. I really respect . . . boundaries." It wasn't the word she wanted, but it was all that came to her. "Anyway, I'm sorry." She held out her hand to shake on it. He took her hand.

"No need for that," he said. "I wasn't offended." They let go of each other. He walked to the door. And then he turned. He did not need to tell her more, but he did not want to make a point of that either. "I just don't get involved in projects," he said.

"Could I ask you for some information, then?" she said.

"Sure," he said and walked back to the desk.

"Could you tell us where we could find someone to design the equipment my friend needs?"

"Tell me again what she is doing."

When she had finished telling him, he took a piece of paper from his notebook and made a series of sketches, precise as drafting, sharply defining the problem.

"What she wants to do is this." He explained the drawings to Sylvia Warren, pointing to diagrammatic objects where she had given him Mildred Latham's ideas. "And this is a list of what she'll need." He made some quick calculations and then wrote. With small numbers in circles, he coded each item in the list to its place in the drawings. On the bottom of the page he wrote the address of a New York City firm. "Tell your friend to say in her order that I asked she get a professional discount."

"This is marvelous of you," Sylvia Warren said. "You've made it so . . . so *tangible.* We really can't thank you enough. Mildred will be boundless in her thanks. Just wait till you meet . . ." But she stopped. "Sorry. Thank you. I mean thank you very much."

"You're welcome," he said. "I'm glad I could help. I used to do this for a living. Well, *molliter cubes.*"

What he had rejected when she had telephoned him was his own old assumption that he would do something because he could do it. But even more he had rejected her passionate investment in Mildred Latham's scheme, the implicit invitation for him to join, for he knew well the sound of endeavor and the enticement to contend for form, and of such investments he would have no part. If it was an odd job that she wanted done, that was OK; she was a decent sort, and he would help her out. Fix a car, learn Latin, rig up some thermocouples to a few clockwork gears and timers—there was no danger in that. He drove home, the nights cold enough now for him not to want to walk in them.

The following week she spoke to him after class about a problem in the wiring. She described what she and Mildred Latham had done during the week. Too anxious to wait, Mildred had driven down to New York and back the same day. They had built as closely as they could to his plan, and when at last they turned on the lamps, after about five minutes the meter reading went up continually to dangerously high levels. Everything else seemed to work. Only the light and heat lamps seemed out of control. They could not work out the problem.

"Are you sure you've got a resistor here?" He pointed to where.

"Yes. Definitely. We double checked. We figured that somewhere we must be making a circuit around that resistor. And yet there must be some resistance somewhere. That's why it takes five minutes before it starts to climb. The current is building. We thought we might be shorting through this little chassis here with the switches on it. But that's as far as we could go."

"I'm impressed," he said. "You know about electrical circuits."

"Not much. Only a little. Mildred's worked with lab equipment somewhat. And me, oh, I've tried practically everything."

"Well, I'm still impressed that you know as much as you do."

She waited.

"Will you help us out?"

"Yes," he said. "I'm obliged to now. If what you say is right, then the fault is in my design, and I can't leave you hanging on that kind of problem. There would be no way for you to fix it. When do you want me to look at it?"

"What's good for you?"

"I'm a free man. The sooner the better I'd guess, if you're doing an experiment with living things. Tomorrow morning? Eight-thirty? I know you're up by eight-thirty."

"Tuesday?"

"Is that not good?" He had heard her patterns speak sooner than she did herself, but she heard them too.

"Tuesday will be just fine," she said firmly. "Eight-thirty. Here's the address." She bent to the desk to write it. "We'll throw in breakfast. How's that?"

"I'll have eaten by then," he said. "But thank you."

He came exactly at eight-thirty and started to work at once. He set up his testing meter and traced through the entire circuit, probing delicately from connection to connection, sometimes stopping to write numbers down. The two women watched him silently. After twenty minutes he said, "Here's the problem." He touched the glass-encased recording thermometer. "The safety fuse in here is larger than I figured. It's pushing current back across here." He ran his finger along the wire to where. "I'll have it fixed in no time." He opened the square black case he had carried in and took from it a soldering gun, some additional tools, and a different resistor. In two minutes he was finished. "Try it now."

Mildred Latham turned the switch, the lamps came on, the meter needle rose and held. For five and then ten minutes he continued to test the circuitry.

"You're in business," he said, turning to look at them at last. The women gave a little cheer.

"May I offer you a cup of coffee, Mr. Harnack?" Mildred Latham said. "At the very least."

"Why yes, Miss Latham. I think I would like a cup of coffee now."

They sat in the parlor of Mildred Latham's house drinking their coffee. She placed a dish of fine, thin cookies near him, but he ate none.

"It's not unlike being a doctor," Sylvia Warren said. "You've even got the little black bag for it. An electronic stethoscope. A thermometer. Instruments. Medicine called resistors and capacitors and whatnot. It's a good analogy. Dr. Harnack, you just made a house call and the patient is doing fine."

Abel Harnack looked down into his coffee, examining it so that he would not have to look up at her. The women looked across at each other blankly.

"I think you'd be very interested in insects, Mr. Harnack," Mildred Latham said. Whatever they had suddenly accidentally gone into, for whatever reasons, Mildred Latham knew to try to take them somewhere else. "They're a lot like machines, like mechanisms," she pushed at him. "No personality. There's nothing you can love in an insect, only think about." Her voice rose a pitch. What had happened? "Their attractiveness is abstract, if you see what I mean, not like with mammals or even birds. It's too easy to slip into *liking* mammals and birds, too easy to start caring about what happens to them. Not so with insects." She looked quickly at Sylvia Warren, stricken. "Insects are fascinating not because of what they might do—they're too perfectly predictable for that—but because of how they work, like beautiful chess games, I suppose, or more like elegant watches."

Abel Harnack looked down deeper into his cup. They were all sliding down. Mildred Latham, bewildered, struggling to pull them out, knocked them further in.

"Yes," she went on, "I'd think they would appeal to someone with your analytical skills and interests. Do you know why some insects can move their wings so quickly?" She started to explain. "There's what amounts to a spring in . . ."

"I'm too busy," Abel Harnack said sharply, looking up, like waking up, interrupting her. Then, quietly, "My head is too full of Latin these days." He stood. "I'll check the circuits." He walked quickly away from them, through the house to the rear room where the experiment had been established. Five minutes later the women followed him. He was working.

"I'm making some changes," he said. "Nothing much. I'll be through soon." In fifteen minutes more he packed up and said goodbye and left.

> Diapause is a means for surviving adverse seasons. It is a method in which the insect enters a state of dormancy, in which all growth changes cease and metabolism falls to a very low ebb, only just sufficient to keep the body alive, so that any reserves of food that are available may last for an extremely long time. This dormant state, or "diapause," may supervene at any stage in the life history of an insect: in the egg, in the young or in the full-grown larva, in the pupa, and even in the adult—where the arrest of growth means the cessation of reproduction. It is not uncommon for diapause to persist for more than one season, and for a pupa to lie over two or three years before it completes its development and emerges. But the record is probably held by *Sitodiplosis mosellana*, one of the wheat blossom gall midges (Cecidomyidae), which passes the winter as a full-grown larva in a cocoon in

> the soil. In this midge dormancy has persisted for as long as eighteen years, and yet in the end the larva has been able to pupate and emerge.

". . . and yet, in the end the larva has been able to pupate and emerge." He reread the line. He could hardly believe it.

Halfway home from Mildred Latham's he had turned and driven back the other way, to the library. She had spoken of the perfect predictability of insects, used those exact words. Was it just an expression, or did she mean exactly that? She was knowledgeable about these things, certainly; but could she have meant precisely what she said, the "perfect predictability" of insects? Now he wanted to find out. He had not felt this important need to know something for a long time. For Abel Harnack, *a long time* had come to mean *since before.*

In the library he began with the *Encyclopædia Britannica* for general information and then moved on to more complete texts. He browsed in them and then settled on *The Life of Insects.* He read the first two chapters and then turned to the index to find "diapause." That was what she was experimenting with. Incredible. He shut the book and rose from the table to take it and the two others to the checkout desk. And there they were again, the two women together as he had left them that morning.

"Why, Mr. Harnack," Sylvia Warren said. "How soon our paths cross." And then she wanted to take it back, to unsay the playfulness; he was not a playful man, and she forced him, and that was no good. Mildred Latham stood by and examined his books.

"Insects," he said to them, holding the books up. "You made me curious about some things about them."

"Wonderful," she said. "Let me help you learn about them whenever you need help." He nodded.

"We're here for the Books-Sandwiched-In program. Every Tuesday at noon," Sylvia Warren said. Absurdly, she wanted him to know that he wasn't being followed.

"Have a nice time," he said and nodded again and walked past them to the checkout desk. He did not care why they were in the library. He had taken a leap he could not have imagined three hours before. Now his mind was elsewhere, closing in. Closing down.

And the winter came on.

Through it Abel Harnack stayed diligently at work upon his Latin, moving comfortably from the ablative absolute through the passive periphrastic to the declension of comparatives to such esoteric elements as the conjugation of *eo* and the constructions of place and time. His vocabulary grew. The system of the language pleased him. And little by little, through what they studied, through what Sylvia Warren would read to them and explain, he came to a feeling for the Latin tone and style of mind, the stoic and heroic or vicious and yet always urbane Latin of the Golden Age and beyond. And, so far as he would ever go into such things, he came to a feeling, limited and tentative, for the vast and tumultuous whirligig of ambitions and acts that the Latin language had shaped and was shaped by. Cicero on the nature of friendship, Horace longing for the simple country life on his Sabine farm, what Pliny thought of the races, Vergil creating a history.

From the greatest to the smallest concerns of the nation or of all humanity, from the most angry denunciations to the most outrageous flattery and groveling, a profound decorum permeated it all, a sensibility to order that resonated in the culture even when there was no order, only the persisting, fading dream of it, the pretense of it, of order that contained the violence of the heart.

For Abel Harnack the ordering of insects was altogether different but more fascinating and better understood. The more he read about them, the more he came to be convinced that the life of insects had achieved the perpetuation of energy in the only way it could ever be achieved. He had been on the right track with his wire net of a machine down in the basement after all, the idea that energy could only be endlessly preserved at its most fundamental and therefore efficient level. But his machine, as simple as it was, was still material first and last; even if it took a million years, the copper and the tin and the silver would oxidize away, back to primary electrons.

Only the insects were perfect, going on in an unending transmogrification of material at whatever pace was possible, like passionless molecules in a chemical formula, the elements of the insects unalterably attached into larger structures as precisely fixed as ions in a bond, as atoms of oxygen in a carbon ring. And even the parts were not necessary to watch each other, so ants could work without abdomens and mantises conspire without heads. Blinded, limbless, the insects could go on. And insects could freeze into crystals and thaw and be insects again.

Abel Harnack saw that the insects, incapable of comprehension or choice, were uninvolved in their fate and thereby had no fate, only function. And he thrilled to see such perfection in the universe, to see that what was prevented for humankind was not prevented in itself, that the dream of endless motion was possible, was *already* possible, though the price was everything else. And most thrilling of all to him was the diapause, where the insect lost even its own necessity and became an extension, a bloom, of the sun itself.

He read deeply about the insects through the winter, but he did not talk much about them to Mildred Latham on the occasions when they met. He listened to her, and he asked questions. But he did not offer. There was an important crossing point that he did not want to have to meet with her, or with anyone. She had meant that the insects were machine-*like.* He meant that they were *machines.* They did not even always need sex to reproduce.

The winter went on. He continued in his new ways, but in his old ways as well. The same hours, the same patterns. Many days he would visit Vivian in the morning unless the weather was too fierce to battle. Once a week he would eat with her family. She was pleased that he was active again.

"You're looking good," Vivian said to him.

"My health is fine. I walk a lot most every day if I can. I get enough sleep. I'm fine."

"That Latin must agree with you," she said. Charles was in the TV room, watching the news. The children thudded about upstairs. Vivian sat with her father in the kitchen, the dinner dishes stacked, the counter and stove already clean and ready for tomorrow.

"It's OK," he said. "I'm learning it."

"And the teacher? What's her name?"

"Miss Warren. Sylvia Warren."

"Yes. What about her?"

"What do you mean?"

"How are you getting on with her?" Vivian looked at him.

"What are you thinking?" her father asked.

"You know what I'm thinking."

"Well, don't," he said. "We're hardly acquainted, hardly even friendly."

"I've seen her. She's not bad looking."

"Stop it, Vivian."

"It's nothing terrible, you know," she pushed on past him, her voice rising with old impatience and new hope. "You're not an old man." She waited for him, prepared to duel, to fight him *for* him. The past was buried; he had a lot of future to think about. But he said nothing. "She's not an old woman." He would not answer her. At last she stood up from the table and walked around the kitchen picking at it, nervous and irritable at his refusal.

"You think you know so much about life," he said to her. "But all you really know about is man and woman, husband and wife."

"Maybe," she agreed. "Maybe that *is* all I know about life. And maybe that's *all* there is."

"*Less,*" he said, suddenly, startlingly, and stood up quickly, stretched to his full height, as if his truth had pulled him up. "*Less,*" he shouted. Then he stooped and kissed her on the forehead. He went through the house and said goodbye to the children and to Charles and went home, above vicissitudes.

The winter deepened. The earth froze and then the sky froze; landscapes and people hunched up, tight and limited, compressed.

About every two weeks he would get a telephone call or a letter beckoning him back to work. Even after a year the offers and the requests continued. His skills had been special, even rare, and so he had continued to be remembered. Sometimes, now, he would give a day or two to the technical problems of old friends. But he knew what limits were, and stayed within them.

In January he signed up for the second semester of the Latin course. The original class of eleven had shrunk to eight by the end of the first semester, and now only five, including himself, had signed up to go on. Five was the minimum. With fewer than five students, the course could not be offered in the extension college curriculum. But he did not sign up as a favor to her. Latin had come to serve him in the way that he had wanted, and if there had been no greater reason to begin than that, then there was now no greater reason to stop.

He won a judgment against General Electric in a patent infringement suit that he had begun five years before. He put the sizable settlement into a common savings account and left it alone.

The storms turned February thick, the snow wet and heavy. Once, when a major transmission line went down, he battered his way to Mildred Latham's with a small, powerful generator and hooked it into her house system so that the light and the heat for *Vendalia tarda* would not go out.

He went on. His days—decorous, predictable—filled up. He had come so very far from a year ago to this sublime calm that he could dare to test himself against memory. Cautiously he would open the door to his empty house that day, to Estelle gone, and would wait for the wave that once had tumbled and suffocated him in the bitter surf of chaos to burst against the clever bulwark he had devised. He would feel the power of the wave on the other side strain and shudder and subside, die and recede. If in his life any longer there was such a thing as pleasure, *that* was pleasure.

At the very end of February after class, before leaving the building, he stopped at the "Boys" room. The sign was still the first one, blue lettering on white porcelain, that had been mounted on the door when the school was built forty years earlier. Vivian had gone to this school. His grandchildren went here now. Outside the wind blew across the parking lot, not quickly or strongly but with steady pressure, weakening slowly what it pushed against, rather than knocking it down. The snow had melted and frozen and melted and frozen into a moon terrain, ripped, pocked, sharp-ridged and uneroded. Nearly to his car, he dimly saw Sylvia Warren on her knees by hers. Her arms were extended forward, her hands flat against the rough ice, her forehead resting against her car door.

He labored through the wind to her.

"Miss Warren," he shouted. She looked up.

"I must have fallen. The footing is treacherous." She looked to him as if she were resting, her eyes quiet. He waited for her to get up, but she stayed.

"Let me help you." He bent to her and took her under her arms.

"Yes," she said. "Please. I'm having trouble." Then she was standing. She had cut her knees.

"Are you all right?"

"A little shaken." She opened the car door and he helped her in.

"Are you sure? Do you want me to drive you home? You could get your car tomorrow."

"No," she said. "It was just a fall."

"He's a very nice man," Mildred Latham said. "He's certainly intelligent. He's quiet, but he'd got keen insight. And he's gentle. That's always a good sign."

"A good sign of what?" Sylvia Warren asked her. They were in her apartment. Barely audible Bach floated about, the volume of the sound inappropriate for the size of the music. "For a proper husband? Do you mean, Mildred, that you're still thinking about getting married?"

"Me?" Mildred Latham actually shouted. "Me? *You.*" But Sylvia Warren was laughing; of course she understood that Mildred Latham had meant her then, and had meant her for nearly twenty-five years.

"You're still trying to get me married."

"It's not that, really. We've talked about that. It's just that I can still never understand why you never did. You're so attractive." She trailed off into the Bach.

"I'm not about to change my life, Mildred. Or have it changed. It works pretty well as it is. And don't you do anything to make Abel Harnack nervous. He doesn't want involvements. I told you about him. He's a specially nice person to be with. Just leave it at that."

"I wasn't going to *do* anything, Sylvia. I'm not a fool or a child."

But the subject was closed. Sylvia Warren got up to make them both some tea. Once she had tried, in an act of disciplined imagining, to picture her life differently; but what would it mean to be a wife? A wife to Abel Harnack? The idea was vacant, empty, the vision of it impossible to form, the thought itself wrong, a disvaluing of themselves as they were. They were, all three, becoming good friends. Even if—*if*—life could have offered more, it did not *require* more. And she would not relinquish herself into new passions, whether offered or not. She enjoyed Abel Harnack's interestingness; she enjoyed the civility of their union. It was enough. Another pleasure.

By the beginning of April the experiment with *Vendalia tarda* had failed. The eggs had not hatched; they had not been brought out of diapause.

"But the eggs are still alive, aren't they?" Abel Harnack said. "Maybe they are going to skip a year, or even two."

"Then what do you propose—that we just let the experiment go on?" Mildred Latham walked slowly about the caged eggs, still shining ticks of matter, inert but glowing, undetermined yet. "For another year. Or another and another. Then leave the whole contraption to the university after we're all gone?" She flung her hand over the apparatus, wiping it out, her disappointment blurring it like a damp rag.

"Yes," Abel Harnack said.

He had come to supper with them. Again. The suppers they had begun to share had gone well, the talk always about Latin and insects, photography and travel and the measurable nature of things—how an electron microscope worked, why plastic took its shape, the use that windmills could have, the distance to stars.

"Our own Royal Society," Sylvia Warren had called them, even just that evening, even with the failure of *V. tarda.* Now, supper complete, coffee finished, they stood in the back room of Mildred Latham's house.

"I haven't the heart for it," she said. "Or the patience. And spring is here. Nearly." She put her arm across Sylvia Warren's shoulders. "Me and Warren here have to get out in the field where we belong. I want to see what *is* hatching from the eggs, not keep on looking at what isn't."

"What will we do with them?" he asked.

"Put them back where I found them, if you like. Would you like that? Come along with us next Tuesday to Triverton and we'll show you."

He agreed.

The natural world of Triverton, the varying terrain of streams and bogs, upland meadows and woods blending from pines to hardwoods, was as unknown to Abel Harnack as an automobile engine might be to most others. One knew *about* meadows and bogs as one knew *about* engines, which was not the same as knowing a thing in itself, the way Abel Harnack could picture actual steel-hot valves opening and closing and the oily black rocker arms compressing and releasing; or the way Mildred Latham would envision the translucent apical cells at the root tip of the skunk cabbage dividing and expanding down into the grainy earth. But here, where the life of things was objectifying fact, where the network, not the element, was the reality, he had never been. Now, late, he had come to a new boundary.

Bloodroot, hepatica, fiddleheads, the lance-sharp buds of beech, the crusted egg-cases of the mantises, fungi fruiting under the powdery bark of rotten trees, tiny mosses greening up, a kestrel darting through the trees, a rare shrew, waterstriders already dimpling the quieter waters. But it was too late for him to know this world as they did, like an elixir, like a potion. He watched them as they ranged widely ahead of him, tracking wonder; the older woman heavy, the younger woman firm, lithe, and effective. From where he watched them, she looked like a young girl, prancing and excited. Both of them did that day, the place transfiguring them.

"Mr. Harnack," Sylvia Warren called back to him. "Come and see this." Mildred Latham was bent down into the grass. As he approached she stood up with a small snake in her hand. She grasped it behind the head and with her other hand held it by the tail and extended it.

"*Thamnophis ordinatus,*" she announced. "The common garter snake. Are you familiar with this?"

"No, I'm afraid not. This is out of my world."

"It's a beautiful thing, a snake. You see here, on the belly, where the single scales stop and the double scales begin? That's the start of the tail." She told him more about snakes, about the musk gland under the anal scale, about the Jacobson's gland with which some snakes tasted the air, that most snakes were born from eggs, but that *Thamnophis ordinatus* was born live like man. She dropped the snake gently, and it disappeared with a soft snap into the grasses. For a moment they all three looked at one another. The sun intensified, the slight breeze rustling the still winter-dry fields. Crows called distantly. The scent of the loosening earth rose all around them like a fume. "I am deeply moved by all of this," Mildred Latham said. Her eyes glistened. Sylvia Warren took her arm and moved off with her.

The day darkened quickly as only April can, going from a bright blue glory to a dirty squall gray. The first light mist of rain caught them far from where they had parked the car, and far from each other. The women waved him to them. When he got to them they hurried him into the woods to an enormous green-black spruce. They lifted the lower branches up from the ground, like lifting the hem of a floor-length dress.

"Go in," Mildred Latham said to him. He got to his knees and crawled in and they followed. Inside, the heavy smell of the spruce was dazing at first, then liquidy, like breathing underwater. Inside it was dark, but enough light came through the infinite hatchwork of the needles. The rain increased, but they were dry. Years of soft brown spruce needles cushioned them.

"It was time to eat anyway," Mildred Latham said. She took from her knapsack a thermos of coffee and a package of thick ham sandwiches on dark bread. "I'm glad for the rain. I love this, getting under this tree, eating here safe from the weather, safe from everything. But you need the rain to make it count, so to speak." She passed around the sandwiches and the cup full of coffee. They ate and spoke a little about their day so far: the extremely early wood duck they had seen, the witchhazel scrub tree that had not cast its seed before the winter, the wild ginger already well started. The year was coming quickly.

"Well, Mr. Harnack, what do you think?" Sylvia Warren asked him.

"It's all very pleasant, Miss Warren. And quite a new experience for me."

"It's always going on," Mildred Latham said. "Winter, spring, summer, fall." She finished the cup of coffee and poured another and handed it to him. And then she said, "I could stay here. On days like this. And other days. I feel like I could stay here forever. Just set up under this spruce and go on until I died here."

"Yes," Sylvia Warren said. "I've had that feeling. Here. But other places too. And sometimes when I'm painting. Or playing music. Or reading Vergil." She laughed. He was startled. Her laughter, always so soft and easy, echoed in his head now, sharply, like a volley of sound shot into him. It was as if he had been told a great and shocking intimate secret, as though what she had told him was safe with him, would not matter though told to a man to whom nothing would ever matter again.

He did not know what to say, or that he could say anything. He understood what the women meant, but there was nothing in his own life he could gauge it by—except his life with Estelle, and he would measure nothing more by that.

He raised the thermos cup of coffee to his mouth and then, as with an attack, he jerked and the coffee spilled. Time sagged. The spilled coffee fell as slowly as life itself, a languid cascading moment, leaving time enough to think of everything before the liquid hit his knee. Time to understand that he had built his life upon defense again after all, but that there were gigantic subterranean waves of memory too strong for any barrier. He had betrayed himself. In the sudden discovery that the fortifications have been breeched, that the enemy is streaming in through the jagged rent, the mind twangs between panic and act. The decision made in that moment is the decision, clearly understood or not, from which all the decisions ever after must come.

So too had he once shared in the profound, harrowing, and wordless condition of love, the boundless, shapeless, measureless condition which is not chaos though it cannot be formed. In which he too would have chosen to stay forever and had, unlike these women, thought he would stay.

Why had he come here with them? What had they had to lose, or not to lose? He should not have come here with them, into this place of contagion where there was no safety at all, only the dangerous belief that there was.

"Oh," Sylvia Warren said as the coffee hit his knee. It quickly soaked through to his skin, but the heat was out of it. His spasm had passed. He handed her the cup. She drank from it. They finished eating and the weather changed back, as Mildred Latham had predicted. Following the women, he crawled out of the spruce shelter into the cleared April-blue day, with all his old vulnerabilities once again intact.

"As you know," she said to the class, "I do not give a final exam. Your grade will be based upon the work you have done throughout the semester." She went quickly on. "This has been a very pleasant year for me and I hope as pleasant for you. We have gotten to know each other rather well through this school year, and we've gotten to know a lot of Latin. I'm really proud of you. You've done splendidly." She went on with the small valedictory. "I wish that you would continue. Do not stop now, here at the beginning of this great adventure. Perhaps over the summer or next year you will find a means to go further."

He sat forward. She was saying something more than the words.

"I conclude with this from Marcus Aurelius." She gave them the Latin as usual, and then translated: "Then depart at peace with all men, for he who bids thee go is at peace with thee."

"*Vale,*" she said, and left before more than that could be said.

He had at first promised wildly that he would sever himself from the women and from Triverton. He would see them no more, and he would not come back. But he did neither.

To refuse to meet with them upon the terms they had established was pointless. He was interested in their knowledge and in their friendship, their companionship. They were fine people. They had taught him much. He could not allow himself to flee from goodness. For if he started to run he would never stop, and the old terror would return and this time there could be nothing that would stop it. He would go on about his life as he had come to live it since Estelle's death, only now the anger that had been reborn under the great sheltering spruce he would accommodate. The truce he had arranged was his mistake. There could be no truce while the battle still raged and wounded. He would continue to see Sylvia Warren and Mildred Latham as the occasions arose.

And he did go back to Triverton. They had taught him that. He returned often. Sometimes with them, sometimes with the nature-study groups that were conducted there in the summer. And sometimes alone. As now.

He could see them down in the glade of the hill he was sitting on. Mildred Latham was beating through the weeds and grasses with the heavier net in a general sweeping for anything that would tumble her way. Sylvia Warren worked with the lighter net, flicking after butterflies or other insects she might spot in flight. They moved slowly through the large field. Even from where he sat he could tell that they were talking to each other, laughing and touching, giggling like animated schoolgirls, their transfiguring gaiety turning them childlike.

Her blouse was as yellow as the thick goldenrod and the heavy late daisies. Her gray hair had tightened through the summer in the sun, white and mirror-like. He watched their progress, the rhythmic beating of Mildred Latham's net, the short, jabbing, staccato swing of Sylvia's. Every ten feet they would stop and deposit their catch in the jars and vials they carried in their knapsacks. Sometimes Mildred Latham would stop longer and set up her camera with its close-up attachments and take pictures. And then they would move on. Sometimes Sylvia would run in a small circle about Mildred, raising and lowering her arms like a butterfly herself. Once, even, Mildred Latham ran after her to try and catch her in her net.

Sylvia came to a tree stump wide enough to stand on. She jumped up on it and, flinging wide her arms, her net still in one hand, declaimed to the multitudinous sea of wildflowers and weeds, to the far hill, to the wide sky. Abel Harnack looked up to where she must be looking and smiled to think how she must think she was so alone. He guessed it would be Horace that she would be telling the world. When he looked down she was gone. Mildred Latham was running, trying to run, to the tree stump. He stood up quickly and hurried down the side of the hill to them.

She was lying flat out when he got to her. Her forehead, her cheekbones, the bridge of her nose were bright scarlet, as if she had been struck by a wide brush across the top of her face. Mildred Latham was by her side, weeping softly.

"What is it?" he said. The women did not show it if they were surprised that he should appear, as if they did not separate this day from others that they had shared. "What is it, Miss Warren?"

"I don't know, Mr. Harnack," she said up to him. "I don't know. I don't know. I don't know."

But she did, and as he swooped down to her and lifted her up in his arms, light as a molted shell, so did he.

At the hospital the doctor said to them, "Are you her family?"

"No," Mildred Latham said. "There is no family. We're her friends. We're very close friends." She was trying to tell the doctor what that meant, but he understood, or perhaps he did not care to know; family or friends, it did not matter to what he would say, would have to tell them. They were sitting in a small office down the hall from the emergency room. They had waited for hours.

"I'm sorry you had to wait so long. We didn't want to tell you nothing, and we didn't want to tell you anything until we were reasonably sure. We don't have many of the tests back yet, but it looks like a form of *lupus. Lupus erythematosus.*"

"Oh," Mildred Latham said, and could say no more.

"What is it?" Abel Harnack asked. The doctor explained: it was a rheumatoid disease related to arthritis or rheumatic fever, but much more serious; it was a blood disease where the body formed antibodies to its own tissues; it was a wasting disease, attacking mostly the connective tissues, but the vital organs as well, so that in time it crippled. So that in time it killed.

"How much time?" Abel Harnack asked.

"It's not predictable," the doctor said. "The disease is characterized by sudden periods of remission and then equally sudden attacks. There are too many variables, too many complications that can develop. We've already started with injections of a corticosteroid hormone. For the inflammation and the pain there's aspirin."

"Aspirin?" Abel Harnack said. It seemed too trivial to be possible. The doctor nodded.

"In the morning she'll go downstate to the university medical center. We'll need to run more tests and to do more examinations. Dr. Felner will be there. He's a rheumatoid specialist. We just can't say, we just can't even guess at what the chances are yet." Then he added, "With *lupus* you never can." They all sat quietly for as long as a minute. "I'm sorry," the doctor said. "I wish there was an easier way to tell you this, but there isn't." He pressed a button on the desk and a nurse came into the small room. The doctor left. The nurse told them where they were going to take Sylvia Warren and when they could see her and what they should bring for her while she would be in the hospital and other things that Mildred Latham did not hear. But Abel Harnack did, and wrote them down.

He did not sleep well. He awoke at four in the morning and dressed and ate a small breakfast and then drove off down to the university three hours away. He drove through the gray morning lightening and thought of *lupus erythematosus. Lupus.* The wolf. How terrible a name for a disease! To call it what it was, the disease that devoured like a ravening animal. But why not? And who was not ill? He did not think back to Estelle or forward to Sylvia Warren or beyond that to himself. He was through with all of that, now. At peace at last.

At the university he went to the library, which would not open for two more hours. He walked about the quiet campus as the sun rose higher and hot as yesterday. He walked to the woods edging the campus, but he did not enter them—just as a year before, had he been here, at this place, he would not have entered them, although, two days ago, he would have gone in to see what he might see. Not now. Now he knew that there was nothing to see anymore. The quickening heat burned off the slight wisps of steamy dew until, at nine, the day was as clear as it would be.

He had decided to be beaten no longer. He had come here to the library to do what he had once always done, which was all he could do—mend, fix what was broken, make better, improve. Try.

He took his little Latin and swung it like an axe, chopping rough, splintered pieces out of a thousand years of words, hewing for her as best he could a gift that should say in language better than his own what he would have her know. But there was no better language.

In the great glass cube of the university library he found his material, mostly from PA 6164 to PA 6296 on the third floor, the quiet east wing. Knowing too little to manage it, he set about piecing together a statement. Through collections, anthologies, and book after book of the Loeb Classical Library series of Latin faced by a page of English translation, he scrambled like a man on a canted, rock-strewn plain, no two steps certain. He would claw through pages of the English and, finding a passage, he would transcribe the Latin across from it.

> And indeed in my opinion, no man can be an orator complete in all points of merit, who has not attained a knowledge of all important subjects and arts.

Thus Cicero mocked him, but he wrote it down:

> *Ac, mea quidem sententia, nomo poterit esse omni laude cumulatus orator, nisi erit omnium rerum magnarum atque artium scientiam consecutus.*

His notes piled up. Some appeared before him that he could not account for:

> *Nigro multa mari dicunt portanta nature, monstra repentinis terrentia saepe figuris, cum subito emersere furenti corpora ponto.*

But what could he do with that?

> Many fearsome things, they say, swim in the black sea—monsters that ofttimes terrify with forms unlooked for, when suddenly they have reared their bodies from the raging deeps.

Could her infinite Vergil offer him no better? Frequently his eye alone drew him onward, as if directed and compelled by a spirit in him:

> Just when the farmer wished to reap his yellow
> Fields, and thresh his grain,
> I have often seen all the winds make war,
> Flattening the stout crops from the very roots;
> And in the black whirlwind
> Carrying off the ears and the light straw.

He plucked at the golden fruit where he could, often reaching for it and missing it and lurching on.

> I am minded to sing of bodies to new forms changing;
> Begin, O you gods (for you these changes have made),
> Breathe on my spirit and lead my continuous song.

But it was too late for evocations.

He struggled on, Tibullus, Ovid, Propertius, Lucan, and the names of those he had no knowledge of at all, poets who clung to Being by the fragment of a stanza. He willed himself on.

Lucretius:

> Like children trembling in the blinded dark
> and fearing every noise, we sit and dread
> the face of light, and all our fears are vain
> like things the child has fancied in the dark.

Horace:

> Thaw follows frost; hard on the heels of Spring
> Treads Summer sure to die, for hard on hers
> Comes Autumn, with his apples scattering;
> Then back to Winter tide, when nothing stirs.

Catullus, her beloved Catullus:

> If a wished-for thing and a thing past hoping for
> should come to a man, will he welcome it not the more?
> Therefore to me more welcome it is than gold
> That Lesbia brings back my desire of old
> My desire past hoping for, her own self, back.
> O mark the day with white in the almanac!
> What happier man is alive, or what can bring
> To a man, whoever he be, a more wished-for thing?

From his storm of notes he hammered together a document, banging on it, adding and arranging until the pen at last stumbled from his hand. He pushed back from the books and considered what he had made. He read it, the Latin, which he could not understand, breaking in his teeth. The morning had passed. He picked up his pen and, winning and losing with every stroke, wrote to her for himself in his own voice:

> which is to say we are all as susceptible to death, as are the insects. Death is as absolute for humans as for midges. When metabolism ceases, autolysis begins, in *Homo sapiens* or in *Vendalia tarda.* If there is comfort anywhere, it is in truth, whatever the truth, and in this, the act of these words.

Then he got up and took his paper and walked out, leaving everything there just as it was.

Mildred Latham was with her when he came into her room. She looked well enough, though still marked by the red insignia. It looked like a birthmark. She had been told. He handed her the paper. She read it and wept and then dried her eyes and smiled, looked up at him beside her bed and nodded once. And together they settled down to wait for the long night surely coming on.